BEAUTIFUL LIES

A DARK SECRET SOCIETY ROMANCE

ALTA HENSLEY

STASIA BLACK

Special Thank you to our editor, Maggie Ryan, and our wonderful beta readers.

And to our cover designer: Deranged Doctor.

THE ORDER OF THE SILVER GHOST

Requests the honor of your presence

———

MR. SULLIVAN VANDOREN

———

As we prepare for the celebration of *The Trials of Initiation*

SATURDAY THE EIGHTEENTH OF JANUARY

At half past Midnight

OLEANDER MANOR

109 Oleander Lane

Attendance mandatory

1

It was too sunny to bury a body today.

It should be raining, overcast, the classic cliché funeral scene. Instead, the bright light that shone from the cloudless sky risked revealing every dark shadow lurking in all of our souls. And I do mean *all* of our souls. There wasn't an innocent person standing around my father's grave, except maybe my younger sister Jasmine. But give our fucked up, rich society time... she was doomed as well.

Old money, Southern secrets, and proper etiquette were nothing more than poisons that would ruin us all.

The rays of light shining through the large weeping willow trees caused us to squint which seemed fitting in this situation. We stood with stiff spines and sour dispositions as we said goodbye to a man we barely knew. We were all nothing but strangers surrounded in the fragrance of magnolia blossoms and sticky sweat while mosquitoes feasted on our blue, silver spoon-fed, blood.

"Though I walk through the valley of the shadow of death, I will fear no evil," the pastor recited like he had done a million times in his morbid career.

But we *should* fear the evil.

That's the problem with all these people in their black designer suits and ridiculously expensive dresses. They fear nothing because they feel they're invincible. They feel they're protected from suffering and misery simply because they're rich.

And yes, I most certainly walk amidst death's shadow. Every step I make is one step closer to losing the person I once was. I will soon be nothing but a shell... just like my father.

My sister reached for my hand and gripped it tightly. Anyone watching us would assume it was an act of two siblings giving each other comfort. But the truth was that Jasmine held me in place. She knew I didn't want to be there. She knew I wanted to walk away and never look back. She knew I felt nothing but hate and contempt. For a teen girl, she was more perceptive and aware than all the rest of these narcissistic assholes who pretended to be my father's friends.

I was there for her, and only her, and thank God she reminded me of that fact before I bolted. My resolve weakened with every syllable of the pastor's ceremony.

My mother stood on the other side of Jasmine, stoic in her black, lace dress that cost a fortune, no doubt. This was her moment. Her chance to play the grieving widow she had surely orchestrated in her mind several times to make sure she performed her role perfectly today. She dabbed at her eyes, but I knew it was all for show.

Sadness was not an emotion a single person felt this day.

Although I could be wrong...

Maybe there was a mistress or two who circled the coffin who truly grieved... grieved their meal ticket, that is.

It wasn't like we hadn't seen this death coming. My father had been dying for a long time, all by his own doing. You can't smoke cigars every day, drink whiskey like water, pop pills for sweet dreams, and not expect your insides to become cancerous. Although his insides had truly become toxic the minute he'd become a man in our society's eyes and took over the family steel manufacturing business.

And now it was my turn.

I was expected to do the same.

Today, as they lowered my father's coffin into the ground, I would be expected to sign over my soul to the devil. I was to be initiated into a secret society in order to keep my family business and all the wealth associated with it.

The Order of the Silver Ghost waited for me.

Tonight was supposed to be the beginning of my Initiation.

My Trials of Initiation.

And even though I had just buried my father... the Order waited for no one.

"I hope they have everything ready for the wake by now," my mother said as we sat in the limo leading the procession to our house. She twisted her white handkerchief and darted her eyes from one window to the other. "With your father now gone, the help has gotten lazy. I never did rule with an iron fist like he did, and they know it."

"I'm sure everything's fine, Mama," Jasmine said softly, patting my mother's thin leg.

"I specifically asked for lemon tarts to be there. They were your father's favorite. But I didn't remind Ms. Cooper this morning, and you know how her memory is getting."

"I reminded her," Jasmine reassured. "The

lemon tarts will be set up, and everything for the wake will be perfect. Don't worry, Mama."

"Yes, God forbid we don't have the lemon tarts," I mumbled as I reached for the vodka bottle and tumbler hosted by the limo.

"Sully..." My name oozed off her tongue in her usual disapproving way. "Do you really think it's wise to be partaking this early?"

"I just buried my father today. I think I'm owed a drink, thank you very much." Just to really stick it to her, I poured the vodka all the way to the rim.

"Especially with what you have to do." She kept squeezing her handkerchief as she pursed her lips. "You have a very important..." She paused and lowered her voice as if the driver would overhear us, and she would be accused of breaking the sacred secret. "*Engagement* tonight."

"Yes, Mother. I'm very aware of my *engagement* this evening."

"Then do you think it's a good idea to drink? I would think you'd want to stay sharp and distinguished."

I chuckled as I took a large swig of the vodka. I held the liquid in my mouth longer than normal just so I could feel the burn. "Distinguished? Is that what you call the ritualistic, barbaric, and fucked up Initiation to join a secret society that should have died off ages ago?"

My sister reached for my hand and squeezed it as a way to silently chastise me.

"It's time you step up and be the man of this family, Sully," my mother said as she scowled at the drink in my hand. "With your father gone—"

"I know exactly what has to happen now that Father's gone," I snapped. "It doesn't mean it's not fucked up."

Jasmine squeezed my hand again. We were brought up not to curse, not to disrespect our elders, and frankly... not to think for ourselves. So, I knew she had to be uncomfortable with how this conversation was going.

"What is *fucked up*," my mother said, repeating the curse in an oddly elegant way, "is your refusal to accept who you are. Who you were born to be. You've always resisted, and I can't figure it out for the life of me. When you ran off to California, I thought it would just be a matter of time for you to realize all you were leaving behind in Georgia." She glanced out the window and stared at the large houses with perfectly landscaped grounds common to Darlington—a town I despised. "But regardless, you have returned home now, and it's time you step up."

"Even if it's not what I want to do?" I asked as I took another sip of my drink.

"And what's the alternative?" she snapped as

she turned her flushed face, with wide eyes toward me.

She better be careful. All the visible facial expressions will cause her to need Botox sooner than she has scheduled on the books.

"We lose everything? Is that what you want? Do you want us to lose the business? The house? All our money? Will you not be satisfied until your sister and I are left out on the street penniless? Will that make you happy finally?"

"No, that's not what I want, which is the only reason I'm here."

She went back to staring out the window. "Yes, I know. Money means nothing to you, but it does to us. Your sister would have to stop attending Darlington Academy, and we'd have to leave everything we know. If you don't do this Initiation and become a member of the Order of the Silver Ghost, then we lose everything your father, and his father, and his father and so on worked so hard to build."

"I don't need to be reminded of the stakes," I said. "But did you ever ask if this is what I wanted? I don't want this business. I don't want to be here and run it. I want nothing to do with all this."

"But I do," Jasmine finally spoke up. "I know you've always hated what Daddy does, but... I want to keep VanDoren Enterprises intact. I can't inherit it like you can, but I want it. So, if you don't want to do this for you, then at least get the business for me."

My sister had never asked me for anything. Well, unless you count all the times she begged me to try to get along with our parents. Jasmine was different than anyone else. She was good, innocent, and simply pure at heart. Even as a teen, she hadn't lost the part of her that made me love her so much. So, for Jasmine to cut in and speak her mind, it had me take pause and listen.

"I understand you don't want to be in the Order," she said in her calm and soothing voice. "I can't even imagine what you'll have to go through. If the rumors are true... well, I don't blame you for not wanting to be part of it."

Our mother opened her mouth to interject but Jasmine raised her hand to quiet her.

"But Mama is right. We'd have to completely start over if you don't do this. The business can only be handed down to a member of the Order and first male born. And the house, our assets, basically everything is tied up and controlled by the business. My trust fund wouldn't last long."

She took a deep breath as she glanced out the window for a brief moment.

"This isn't just about the money, Sully. I want to keep the family business. It means a lot to me. Please."

"I know," I said calmly, trying to soften my temperament. "Which is why I came back from California. And as much as I fucking hate it, it's why I'll go through the Initiation." I looked Jasmine straight in the eyes so she could see just how serious and committed I was. "I'll do this for you."

2

SULLY

The Oleander Manor.

My new home for the next 109 days.

Opulence, wealth, and a history so rich in cloaked secrets you could hear the steps of our forefathers still roaming the rooms today. I used to love this estate as a child until I learned to detest it. It used to be a special place my father took me to back when I thought the man walked on water. I had friends I would play with while my father conducted business. It all seemed so normal... on the surface.

But beneath the murky waters of a membership open only to the kings of Georgia lurked pure evil. No way to dress up that fact.

I went from wearing all-black attire to all white in a matter of hours. I hated the white tuxedo look which was the required dress code for the evening. Actually, I hated being in a tuxedo period. I much preferred worn jeans and a cotton shirt. When I was forced to wear a tuxedo or expensive suit, I felt like nothing more than a dressed-up Ken doll.

"I'm surprised you actually agreed to your Trials of Initiation," Montgomery Kingston said, as he approached with two drinks in hand, offering me one with a smile. He wore a silver cloak that only the members of the Order of the Silver Ghost wore, and it was odd to know that, although he was my friend, he was no longer exactly the same as me. He had completed his Trial. He was a full-fledged member now. "I expected you to be a no show."

"If I could be anywhere else, I would," I said, grateful to drink from the liquid courage provided. "Any tips on how to survive this since you just suffered through it?"

"Don't count the days, because trust me, 109 days is a long fucking time," Montgomery answered. "And I'm not saying you have to fall in love and want to marry the girl you're paired up with like I did with my belle, but you have to get along. You're a team whether you like it or not. It's the only way to pass these Trials. And trust me, some of them are beyond brutal."

"I don't see that happening. Let's be real," I said.

"You lucked out with Grace. You know as well as I do these belles are nothing but high-priced hookers. They're here for a payday and nothing more."

"The same could be said about us, man." Montgomery shrugged. "It's all how you look at it."

The rest of my friends, and fellow recruits, walked up to join Montgomery and me since we were approaching the midnight hour. It was no secret I wasn't a fan of Darlington, of the Oleander Manor, or The Order of the Silver Ghost, or basically anything of late.

But I liked these guys. We had history together and had grown up side by side. We each marched to our own beat, but I knew they were good guys deep down. If I had to do this Initiation, I was happy I didn't have to do it completely alone. Montgomery Kingston, Beau Radcliffe, Rafe Jackson, Walker St. Claire, and Emmett Washington were as close to brothers as I would get.

"You ready for this?" Rafe asked.

I shrugged. I could keep standing here and bitching, or I could power through it. I was pretty sure the guys were sick of my pissed-off attitude and didn't need or want to hear any more of it.

"We all gotta do it," I said as I finished the last of my drink and placed the glass on a nearby table.

"What's it like being a true member of the Order now?" Emmett asked Montgomery.

"Odd," he answered. "To be honest, it doesn't feel that much different other than I don't have to worry about jumping through all the hoops and tests to get where I am anymore. I know I'm expected to be at all the events from now on, which frankly, I'm not thrilled about. I don't want to be part of Sully's Trials at all. I think it sucks that I'm going to have to witness them. But it is what it is. The price I have to pay, I suppose."

"Just don't become like those monsters," I said as I closely watched the white grandfather clock that mastered the pristine white ballroom. "You're not an Elder yet, but still. Don't emulate them."

"Never," Montgomery stated firmly. "I will not become my father. I won't repeat history. This Order needs an overhaul, and hopefully once we all become members, we can help make that happen."

Our conversation was interrupted when the clock struck midnight. The familiar hammer strike of twelve chimes echoing through the room was accompanied by the Elders and their canes. With each chime of the hour, the canes beat in cadence against the white floor.

"Bring in the belles," one of the Elders demanded after the twelfth strike of his cane.

The recruits lined up with me in the center of the room as we had done with Montgomery during his Initiation. Montgomery walked over to join the members all draped in eerie silver cloaks. I stood at attention and waited. At least I knew what to expect and wasn't operating in the blind so far.

The silence in the room changed when the belles and the clicking of their heels entered the ballroom.

Twenty young women.

Twenty beautiful lies stood before me.

As they entered the room, they positioned themselves in a single file. It reminded me of some fucked-up version of a Miss America pageant. Contestants on display. All hoping to be chosen as the winner.

Long-flowing ball gowns of a multitude of colors seemed to dwarf the women. They didn't belong in the expensive garments any more than I belonged in the white tuxedo, and it was obvious in their uneasiness. We were in costumes surrounded by men in silver cloaks, and anyone could read it in their eyes, their posture, and could smell it in the air.

They didn't belong, and they each knew it. They were just praying we wouldn't be able to tell if they dressed and acted the part. But the aroma permeating the air gave it away...

Fear had an odor, and it reeked.

"Display the belles," the Elder commanded with a beat of the cane.

Another Elder began the procession of the belles by leading them one behind the other through the ballroom. He walked them in front of the cloaked Elders first, then the members, and then to us.

They repeated the act three times, circling the room as if they were marching soldiers flanking the ballroom under strict order, although their military uniforms were replaced by gowns worn by true Southern belles.

Except these Southern belles were frauds. Liars. Some of the women even struggled walking in the heels that were provided. Fish out of water.

"Sullivan VanDoren," the Elder called out as the women lined up once again before us. We hadn't moved, but simply watched the parade of deceit. "It is time for you to choose the belle."

The Elder who had been leading the procession of belles walked over to where I stood and opened his fist. Resting on his palm was a black satin ribbon.

I needed zero instruction to know what to do next as this process was clearly laid out in our handbook that ruled over every breath we took. Plus, it wasn't long ago I watched Montgomery as he was offered the same color ribbon.

Taking the ribbon, I struggled not to roll my eyes or go tell them to go fuck themselves. I then walked up to the line of women and began what was called "the touching of the pearls".

I knew I was expected to approach each female and briefly touch the pearl necklace they all wore. I was to make a show of it. Add some flavor and spice to the ritual.

I was supposed to take this act seriously. I was choosing the belle who would change my future forever. I was supposed to honor and value this time of "pearl touching" as if it were one of the most important decisions of my life.

But let's be real. A whore is a whore regardless of what color dress she wore to conceal that fact.

I quickly walked the line and touched the pearls so the Elders couldn't say I didn't and, therefore, fail my Initiation before it even truly started.

Once I had, I stood back and observed the line of women. They all watched my every move, and frankly, they all looked the same in my eyes. Pretty faces, hopeful eyes, and everyone dolled up with makeup, oversized eyelashes, hairspray, painted nails, and everything I hated.

Fake beauty.

If I had walked into a bar and been presented with the same women, I would leave alone, or maybe pick up the bartender because at least she would be real. But I didn't have that option here, so I would have to choose someone.

"Sully VanDoren, you are to choose a belle," an Elder prodded with a bang of his cane. At least he wasn't calling me "Sullivan" which I fucking hated.

All right then, fine. Which of these ladies was the most deserving? Who was the epitome of what this Order and our entire wealthy society of pricks and princesses stood for? I needed to pick the poster child so I could be the Golden Boy.

I needed to pick the complete opposite of who I would choose in my normal life just to constantly remind myself that this sick nightmare wasn't normal, and it was all a guise... a game. So, I would play their game.

Let me find my Barbie since I was their Ken.

My sick sense of humor gave me some pleasure as I scanned the women again and focused my attention on the female with the classic Southern Belle appearance. Long blonde hair, blue eyes surrounded in thick lashes, pouty lips with peach lipstick that shone beneath the chandelier lights, and to top it all off... she wore a pink dress. Yes, she was the perfect vision of a Georgia Peach.

My mother would be so proud.

Drinking her in from head to toe, I also came to an important conclusion.

I could fuck her.

In fact, I might actually get some pleasure out of it since she did have a rocking body.

Not wasting any more time, I walked up to where she stood and locked eyes with her.

She held my stare and seemed to stiffen her spine as her posture improved. Her eyes narrowed, and I saw her jaw clench.

It almost seemed as if she was silently daring me... yes, that was the feeling I got. She didn't smile or play coy. She didn't flutter her eyelashes or lick her lips. No... I was pissing her off as I examined her like she was a piece of meat.

"I dare you, fucker."

"All right, bitch."

"Game on."

"Game on."

I yanked the pearl necklace hard, not caring or looking as the pearls scattered all around us. Her eyes narrowed even more, but she remained in place and didn't show any emotion other than one of challenge.

Breaking the necklace. An act to show just how easy it is for The Order of the Silver Ghost to give you riches only to take them away. What you believe to be yours can be ruined with such ease. But in my case... it was also to show her I was in control.

Not her.

She better figure that out real quick.

Not wanting to play this game any longer under the eyes of the Elders, I replaced the white that had been on her neck with the color black. Locking eyes, I crossed the ribbon at her throat and pulled tightly... tighter than someone normally would. In fact, I got great pleasure in tugging on that ribbon to the point where her narrow eyes widened.

It was my warning.

Montgomery had told me the key to completing the 109 days was to find a teammate, but I was never good at taking advice. I was different. I saw this Initiation as if I were going to war.

There would be no *us*.

Simply *me*.

I was the General, and this little Barbie would be my soldier. She better stay in line and follow my orders if she knew what was good for her. I certainly would have no issue in teaching her a lesson of what would happen if she crossed me.

Tying the ribbon into a bow around her neck, I heard, "Sully VanDoren, have you chosen your belle for the Trials of Initiation?"

I took a step back from the belle in pink and nodded.

"I have chosen."

3

PORTIA

W hen the invitation arrived two days ago at our run-down double-wide trailer, I thought it had been sent by God and the holy angels above.

I'd always been an optimist. As the oldest of four sisters with barely a dollar to squeeze between us some days, I had to be, or I'd lose my mind.

When one door closes, somewhere a window opens, right?

And now here I was, standing with nineteen other hopeful beauties behind a heavy mahogany door awaiting what I hoped would be a life-changing experience.

I glanced surreptitiously around me. All the other girls were gorgeous. Their make-up and hair were flawless, their gowns steamed to perfection.

Glossy, plump lips. Long eyelashes they fluttered alluringly, like they'd practiced.

My nerves frayed even further. Was I the prettiest here? I had no clue. People had commented about my looks before. I wasn't sure if it was just because I was blonde and blue-eyed or if it was because they thought I was actually pretty. A couple of my teachers had said I should do beauty pageants, but of course we never had the money for that, and Mama was always too sick anyway.

But what would this mysterious "Initiate" think of me? Would he look beyond our powdered facades to try to guess who we were inside?

Then I snorted internally. Who was I kidding? Every guy I'd ever known made snap judgments on looks alone. What was it they said? Men judged a woman and whether they were attracted to her or not within five seconds of meeting her. I believed it.

I'd arrived hours ago after being dressed to the nines in the gorgeous gown dropped off at our trailer, then made up by my three sisters.

I was met at the door by Mrs. Hawthorne. She took one look at me and then gave a nod of approval. Thank God for my sister Tanya and her impeccable skills borne of years fussing with her own hair and make-up and watching YouTube tutorials.

"Finally, one of you arrives looking acceptable."

She ushered me inside and quickly led me up a back staircase to a preparatory room.

While a doctor examined me in a small, spare room on the second floor of the manor, white walls with dark wood floors, empty except for a twin bed, Mrs. Hawthorne grilled me about why I was here and what I hoped to gain if I was chosen.

I was nervous, and when I was nervous, I chattered.

So, I told her all about my sisters. "I'm here for my family. Well, my sisters. I'm the oldest and then there's Tanya, Reba, and LeAnn. My mama loved country music stars, so she insisted on naming her babies after them."

Mrs. Hawthorne looked confused, and I figured maybe it was because she was Scottish, or so I assumed based on her accent, so I explained further. "You know, Tanya Tucker, Reba McIntyre, LeAnn Rimes? They were all big country stars in the eighties and nineties."

"So is Portia a star's name, too?" she asked in her lilting accent.

"No," I looked down. "My daddy named me." An uncomfortable reminder that I had more of my no-good father in me than any of my sweet sisters. His unsettled spirit, his wanderlust, always itching to be anywhere else but where he was—I inherited it all as a pig loves a mud-bath on a hot summer day.

Even the name he gave me—he meant for it to be *Porsche*, like the damn car, but at least Mama intervened and wrote it in a more dignified spelling on the birth certificate. Even when naming his own damn kid he'd already been dreaming about driving off into the sunset and leaving his family behind.

Unlike him, though, when the going got tough, I *stayed*.

I would always stay and fight for my family. No matter what. Because Portia? When I finally looked up what that spelling of the name meant? It stood for: *An offering.* And yes, I would offer my life for my family, happily. Every time.

"Anyway," I continued on brightly. I'd decided a long time ago not to dwell on sad things I couldn't change. "My sisters are the best. I'd do anything for them."

Mrs. Hawthorne's eyebrows narrowed as the doctor worked the speculum beneath the sheet set up to cover my bottom half. I jumped a little at the cold metal but otherwise it wasn't too uncomfortable. The doctor was female, and I appreciated that. She was quiet and had a gentle touch.

"So, you're here for them?"

I nodded, trying to relax. "We're about to get

kicked out of the trailer and my sisters, well, they depend on me for a lot of reasons."

I went on and explained everything, and Mrs. Hawthorne got real quiet.

"They just cut off our electricity again, and we're a month behind on rent after Reba lost her temp job. Then Tanya went and quit working her fast-food job when her boss wouldn't stop making passes at her."

I bit my lip and tried not to shift as the doctor opened the speculum wider inside me. "We were just down to LeAnn's afterschool job bagging groceries, but she's just fourteen and can't get a ton of hours, and it's just minimum wage anyway. My job doing eldercare assistance—well, I just never had a chance to go to college obviously, so it's not like official nursing or anything." I shook my head. "And the bills just keep piling up..."

My family was my responsibility, and I was failing them.

The doctor finished up and left the room without interrupting us.

"Listen here, lassie." Mrs. Hawthorne sat on the bed beside me as I cradled the sheet to cover myself.

"I love these boys like my own kin. The man who'll be doing the choosing, he's a little... rough around the edges. Deep down, he's a good boy. I can't say much more than that, but he could use a woman like you to keep him on an even keel through this. You could help each other. Tell him why you're here. It'll help."

She was talking like she thought I actually had a chance at this. It brought back that little bud of hope I'd barely dared spread any sunshine on.

Could this really be it? Salvation dropped from the sky? Or at least in the form of a stranger in a tux knocking on a door a couple nights ago with an oddly formal invitation, followed today by an extravagant dress and limo?

The truth was, we were out of options. This was our last Hail Mary pass. We'd been riding the edge of the poverty for a few years now, ever since—

But no, not thinking about that right now.

Mrs. Hawthorne got up looking as if she was about to leave. "The doctor will be back with the birth control shot any moment. All that's left is to tell me what you want out of this. What is your greatest wish?"

I paused, not wanting to mess it up. What if it was like a genie wish in the old stories and if you worded it wrong, they'd screw you out of everything you were entitled to because of some unforeseen loophole?

"What did the last girl ask for?" I hedged.

"At first? Money."

"How much?"

"Ten million."

Then I frowned. "Wait, what do you mean *at first*?"

Mrs. Hawthorne paused and then leaned in like it was a secret. "It's never happened before, so don't get your hopes up. But by the end of the trial, she and the Initiate fell in love. She gave up the money and her only wish was to simply be with him."

That sounded romantic... and impractical.

"But you're making me feel as if it doesn't just have to be money. That the Order has power to give me anything I want. Anything?"

"Within means."

I made my request. Which saying out loud, even in a whisper to a woman I felt I could trust, scared me I would jinx everything. Saying it out loud made it real. I was taught as a child you never told someone your wish when you blew out your candles on your cake because it wouldn't come true, so from this moment on, my wish out of all wishes would remain locked away in the impenetrable safe of my soul.

"Can they do that?" I asked.

She nodded. "They've done it before."

I closed my eyes and breathed out in relief,

sinking back against the wall. It would be over, hopefully once and for all.

I looked back up at Mrs. Hawthorne. "Let's do this."

And now here I was, standing and waiting for the choosing ceremony. Waiting behind this mahogany door, praying to be picked by the Initiate. I wanted it so badly. Needed it.

But guys hated needy chicks. I had to be calm, cool, and collected. They were looking for "belles", right? I could be the epitome of a Southern belle.

Refined. Regal. Expensive. Elusive.

Everything I wasn't in real life.

But this was all fiction. A performance, a lie. Wasn't that what rich people were? They sinned just as much as the rest of us, they just didn't have to pay for it. They got to pretend they were above it all.

They got to skip to the front of the line—their greatest sin.

Tonight I'd be one of them. For 109 days I'd play the part.

But only *if* I got chosen.

Then, before I was ready, the door swung open. Some of the girls scuffled briefly to be at the front of the single file line, but I grabbed a spot in the middle. Getting into a girl-fight right out of the gates would not be regal or elusive.

We paraded in, single file. My mouth dropped open a tiny bit as we entered.

It was an intimidating, spotless white ballroom. I'd never seen anything like it. The whole manor was over a hundred years old, probably significantly more. And looking around was like we'd stepped out of time and slipped into a side pocket where it was still a century ago.

Men in pristine white tuxes mingled, cocktails in hand until they positioned themselves in an orderly line. And then there were the men in luxurious but ominous silver cloaks. The sheen of the rich fabric shimmered under the light of the huge gas chandelier. Each of the cloaked men held a silver-topped cane.

One of the men in a cloak demanded for us to be displayed and we arranged ourselves in a brightly colored line, our gowns vivid splashes of color in the otherwise monochrome room.

As we walked in a circle, I searched the room furiously, trying to get my bearings and figure out which of the men in white tuxes was the Initiate of the night.

The men in tuxedos stood at attention, reminding me of soldiers preparing for war. Some watched our procession curiously, but one was just downing his glass of dark amber liquid. He seemed completely uninterested in the proceedings. Jeez, if he was here to support his friend, he was doing a crap job at it.

I hoped it was either the studious looking one or the guy smiling kindly at us like he was trying to encourage us all that we were doing well.

Instead...

It was the drunken lout whom the Elders approached with a small black ribbon and a scowl on their faces as the drunk's empty glass was taken away.

You've got to be kidding me. Him?

My heart sank. He didn't even look like he wanted to be here. He walked unevenly towards the belles and brushed his hand roughly over the pearls at their necks.

When he got to me, I tried to make eye contact with him, to secure some kind of connection between us.

Mrs. Hawthorne had warned me he was rough around the edges. But still I'd expected... well, something more than *this*. And yet, hadn't I just been thinking it was unfair to judge someone based on only a few minutes of interaction?

He barely touched my pearls, never once looking in my face before moving on to the next girl. He seemed to have less and less time for each girl as he went down the line, and my hopes sank even further down into my stomach.

This man was not my hope for salvation.

He was a drunk rich boy with too much money and privilege who'd probably never done a hard day's work in his entire life.

An Elder, obviously trying to reinstate some of the pomp and circumstance of the ceremony, banged his cane on the floor. "Sully VanDoren, you are to choose a belle."

Sully VanDoren. VanDoren... good Lord, I couldn't think of a name that screamed *money* and *privilege* more than that.

Okay, so this obviously wasn't going to work out. I'd have to think of other out-of-the box solutions to my family's problems. Dammit. I'd have to quit doing eldercare. I'd miss my patients, but maybe if I got a lucrative waitressing gig in the city, I could send money back and—

Suddenly Sully stomped over and stood in front of me.

I froze and stared back at him, feeling first like a deer caught in headlights and then getting irrationally pissed when he *continued* doing nothing but standing there.

Did he get off on this? Toying with women?

Was he actually going to choose me? Why on earth?

Even now, he stared like he detested me.

I glared back at him. Yes, when the invitation had first come, it had felt like a godsend.

But now I had the distinct feeling I was looking into the eyes of the devil. This was a man pushed to the edge, on the brink.

I had no idea what the hell had pushed him there. But it seemed obvious he had zero fucks to give. And a man like that was dangerous.

I should have dropped my eyes. Cowered away. Signaled I wasn't for him. That definitely would have been the smart thing to do.

But I didn't do any of that.

I straightened my spine and challenged the devil. Because goddamn him, I was a woman pushed to the brink, too. And screw him for thinking he could make me feel small or cower for even a second before his great and almighty—

Before I could even fully take a breath, he ripped the pearls off my neck.

I blinked in shock.

Holy shit! If the Elders' canes banging hard against the white floor meant what I thought it did… I'd just been chosen.

4

PORTIA

There was no time to consider or reconsider. There were just flashes, images. Crying belles as they were led away, the murmur of conversations among the other members, and us being ushered up the stairs.

Sully and me.

Sully was at my side, but he didn't say a word.

Sex.

Now was the time for the sex.

Mrs. Hawthorne and the doctor had explained what was expected of me, and I wasn't shocked. I liked sex and never got to have near enough of it because I was always run so damn ragged. I'd had boyfriends here and there, but they usually ran off quick enough when they realized I always prioritized my family over them.

Sorry not sorry. Don't ask me to choose between you and my family because you'll lose every time.

So sure, okay, sex.

When I said I would do *anything* for my family, I meant it. And I wasn't a prude.

But as the entire entourage followed us upstairs, it hit me in full. Holy crap—my first time with grouchy Sully VanDoren was going to be very public, voyeuristic sex with a bunch of dudes in cloaks looking on.

And Sully wasn't going to make it easier on anyone.

"So, you all gonna come and watch me fuck her?" he asked the following crowd with a crude laugh. "Is that what gets your old peckers hard? Well, hell, maybe we should do a raffle and sell tickets. Why not get the PTA of Darlington Prep involved?"

Sully slammed open the door to a bedroom and yanked me inside by my elbow. It was more abrupt than painful.

I hoped his sour attitude might shame some of the Elders from following or turn them away, but nope, they all just streamed into the room after us anyway.

The room was large and dominated by an absolutely gigantic four-poster bed. The frame was dark wood, antique, and the intricate scrolling wood-work on the headboard truly stunning. Not that there was much time to study it when I was still being flung all about by Sully's strong grip on my arm.

"You know the rules, Sullivan," one of the Elders said. "The first consummation must be witnessed by all."

"Well, fuck," Sully said sloppily, yanking off his shirt and tossing it haphazardly on the antique settee at the foot of the bed. Several matching plush deep maroon wing-backed chairs were set artfully around the room. Many Elders sat in them, apparently settling in for a show. It only set Sully off more.

"Can't let down the sacred handbook. The halls of the Oleander would shake on their foundations if the first fuck wasn't witnessed by all."

He jammed down his pants and then headed wobbily towards me where I stood hesitantly by the bed.

"Hike up them skirts, baby. I hear we're paying by the hour. What's your rate? How many millions you getting paid to get fucked every which way over the next three months?"

I wanted to slap him.

Any other man who spoke to me like that would have ended up with more than my handprint on his face. He would have been walking home with a shiner.

Daddy taught me how to punch before he ran off. And he passed on his temper.

I glared at Sully. "Are you even sober enough to do the job?" I hissed at him.

I didn't care who was watching or listening. And then I leaned in, because I had a little of the devil in me, too. "Doesn't bother me, cause I get paid either way, limp dick or no."

Well, that got a reaction. His eyes flashed. "You don't want to play with me, little girl."

I climbed up on the bed and laid back, hiking up my voluminous pink dress. Next, I slid out of my underwear. Not a small feat considering how much fabric there was to the gown.

Then I laid there with my legs open, staring at Sully as if daring him.

Okay, inside I was freaking the hell out. But false bravado had gotten me through my share of shitshows in the past, and the sooner this was over, the better.

Sully hesitated a moment, looking down at me.

Behind him, Elders lined the walls, standing like sentries in front of the dark red curtains that hung ceiling to floor. Some had hands in their pants as they watched us; some touched themselves over their robes.

I blinked and refocused my attention back on Sully. The only way I was going to get through this was by concentrating on him and him alone. I arched an eyebrow. "Well, are you going to stick it in or what?"

A few guffaws of laughter came from the peanut gallery, which clearly enraged Sully. And then he walked the few steps to the bed, kicking off his tuxedo pants and boxers as he approached.

My eyes immediately widened. He was suddenly looking not as drunk, and holy hell, one glance down showed he was *very* ready to take care of business.

In fact, I'd never seen any cock so long or thick in my life. My mouth went dry, and it wasn't until he laid a knee on the bed that my eyes flew back to his face.

"So, the whore likes what she sees."

Whore? What a hypocritical son of a—

But before I could make any sort of intelligent rebuttal, he'd put his huge cock at my entrance. I felt my eyes go as wide as saucers at the same time I slickened, readying for him.

Everything I'd learned about this man in the past ten minutes made me despise him.

But my body... well my body hadn't exactly gotten the message. All I heard was that the hottest man I'd ever laid eyes on was currently hovering over me, massaging back and forth over my clit with the most glorious cock of all time and—

I couldn't help the full-body spasm of pleasure as I arched into Sully.

And bastard that he was, he didn't miss it either. A big, satisfied smile stretched across his face.

That damn smile sent another rush of wetness to my center, easing the way for his cock to slide in about half an inch. Oh dear God—

I missed this feeling. Who was I kidding? I'd never felt anything like *this*.

Then again, I'd always dated safe boys. Boys who fucked quick in the back seat of cars and always called the next day.

Not this dangerous heat and angry intensity.

Sully moved the slightest bit, grinding into me so his shaft rubbed down against my clit, and I about lost my damn mind.

"That's right," he rasped. "You lie there and take what I give you."

I wanted to argue. I should bite back with a cutting comment. But then he thrust all the way in, and all I could do was widen my legs and welcome him home.

So, he was an asshole. He was an asshole who was about to give me the best sex of my life. It was a sign of maturity to learn how to compromise, right?

I lifted a leg and hiked it over his ass, trying to draw him in closer.

He liked that, if the way he pulled back and then slammed back in were any indication.

For a second, I thought maybe he'd forgotten the rest of the world and was in it just as much as I was.

Of course, I should have known better. If I'd learned anything about Sully in my short acquaintance, it was that he was a stubborn bastard.

He turned his head back to the group of Elders as he continued fucking me, each time dragging tortuously against my clit and taking me higher and higher.

"This isn't fucking normal, you know that, don't you?" he called to them, never slowing his pace. "Go home to your wives! What are you even doing here? Gathering spank bank material to jack off to later? It's fucking messed up."

I should be appalled he was using having sex with me as an object lesson. If he thought this was all so screwed up, why the hell was he participating? And participating so... damn... *vigorously*?

Oh! I couldn't help my high-pitched gasp when he hit an especially sensitive part that had me lighting up inside. Oh dear *God*, was that the g-spot? I'd always thought it was a myth.

I reached down and grasped the sheets out of desperation, biting back the scream of pleasure wanting to make its way from my throat.

Dear God— It shouldn't be— How did he—

And then all thoughts were blanketed by oblivion as the overwhelming pleasure hit.

My limbs went rigid as I clutched Sully's ass. Wait, when had my hand made it to Sully's ass—oh screw it, it all felt too good. Too good. Sooooo good. Soooooooooo—

I turned my head into the pillow and finally let out the roar of pleasure, closing my eyes so I could fully live in it without anyone ruining the moment.

It went on and on, Sully still pumping into me, harder now.

Rougher.

More wild.

Oh *Godddddddddddddddd.*

Wild like I'd never known, taking complete control of my body, and I gave it over. God help me, I gave in—

Riding and riding the high until it tripped over another peak... until finally, *finally,* I was limp as a ragdoll.

Only then did Sully still, the hot rush of him filling me deep inside.

5

SULLY

The early morning sunlight nearly scorched my eyeballs.

I had no idea what time it was, but there was no way in hell it could already be time to get out of bed. Groaning, I rolled over to my side to put my back to the large window overlooking the manicured grounds of the Oleander.

"Oh good, you're up," I heard a perky voice say from the foot of the bed.

I peeked an eye open to see half the bed already made as if Barbie never even slept in it last night, which I knew she had.

"I'm not," I grumbled as I closed my eye again in hopes I could block out the fact I had fucked a total stranger last night, crawled into a bed with her to sleep like we were a damn married couple, and now we were expected to have after-sex morning chit chat.

"I've been waiting for you to wake up," she said.

"Well, I'm not awake."

"You're talking. This means you're up."

I rolled onto my back and opened my eyes to see Barbie dressed in leggings, a sports bra and tennis shoes. Her blonde hair was pulled back into a high ponytail, and a bright smile was on her face.

"Why are the curtains open?" I placed my arm over my eyes. "It's too bright in here."

"Because we aren't vampires. That, and I hate sleeping with the curtains drawn. I like to wake up with the sun. It's a great way to start the day."

I groaned again, not being able to process her words with the pounding headache I had.

"I didn't want to go through your clothing as you slept, but hopefully you have some workout clothes," she said as I heard the closet door open. "You have running shoes at least. So, that's good."

I didn't say anything. Maybe if I played dead, she would grow tired of me and move on to something else.

"I didn't make the rules," she said, dropping my shoes by the bed.

"What rules?"

"The ridiculous one where I'm not allowed to leave the room unless you're by my side. Apparently, I need a guardian or something." I felt her weight as she sat on the edge of the bed. "I tried to be patient, but the walls are closing in on me."

"Patient for what?" I mumbled as I rolled back over on my side and yanked the blanket up around my face.

"Let's get out of here. I need to go for a run to clear my mind." She shook my leg. "Come on. It'll be good for us."

"No," I stated simply, repositioning my head on the pillow in hopes I could fall back asleep.

"Sully, come on." She patted my leg again. "We can't stay in here all morning."

"We can," I mumbled.

"Sully..."

I remained silent.

"Sully..."

I pulled the blanket over my ear.

"Sully..."

"Go back to sleep until we get our next marching orders from the Elders," I said.

"Come on," she prodded, this time shoving my leg and sounding much less perky. "Get your hungover ass out of bed and come with me. If you don't... I swear to God, I'll walk out that door alone and risk ending this entire Initiation for us both. I'm not one to sit on my butt and do nothing." She yanked the blanket and sheet off me with zero warning.

Her gasp would have made me laugh if I wasn't so annoyed at having the bedding pulled away from my naked body. Clearly embarrassed as her face turned pink, she quickly turned her back to me.

"Get used to seeing me naked, Barbie. I sleep in the buff."

She snapped her head over her shoulder and glared at me. "Don't call me that."

I shrugged as I kicked my legs off the side of the bed and stretched my arms above my head knowing any chance of going back to sleep was futile. "What would you like me to call you? I don't even think I know your name."

Jesus Christ. I fucked this woman and knew absolutely nothing about her other than she was an annoying morning person.

"Portia Collins," she said as she walked over to the closet again. "I'm not your Barbie. I'm not your sweetie; I'm not your baby or darling, or any other demeaning pet name. Call me Portia or nothing at all."

"Barbie suits you," I said as I strode— unashamed of my nudity—toward her.

"Yeah, well... Asshole suits you too, but you don't see me calling you that."

She yanked a t-shirt off a hanger and then threw it in my direction. I could see my lack of clothing unsettled her. She avoided looking down at my cock which was on full display due to morning wood. She dug around in the nearby dresser and found a pair of gym shorts that were then thrown my way.

"Come on, get dressed. Your pudgy gut will thank me for the morning run," she said with a smirk and a raise of an eyebrow.

I instantly tightened my stomach muscles. Pudgy? I had a fucking six pack and she knew it. But damn her for knocking me down a notch and making me feel slightly guilty for my heavy drinking and body neglect as of late. And it wasn't like I could counter insult because this Portia girl was damn near perfect. Her body was tight, toned and curvy in all the right places. But seeing her dedication this morning to keep it that way, told me I had a long 109 days ahead of me.

"A quick run, and that's it," I agreed as I got dressed under watchful and impatient eyes.

"If that's all you got in you," she said with a shrug.

It was too early to banter with her. The morning cobwebs were thick, and my head still pounded. We could at least agree on one thing...

fresh air was needed. This room already felt too small with the two of us in it.

We were out the door and running side by side down the avenue of oaks far quicker than my body was ready. Bourbon still oozed from my pores, and my *pudgy gut* threatened to puke what booze was still inside of it. This was about the last thing I wanted to do but giving Little Miss Fitness Queen the upper hand wasn't an option either.

"Are we going to discuss last night, or just pretend I wasn't balls deep inside of you?" I began, concentrating on not huffing and puffing after each word.

"You really can be an ass, you know," she said, not sounding winded in the slightest. She even picked up the pace, which I begrudgingly matched.

"Why? Because I say it like it is?"

"Fine. What do you want to discuss?" she asked.

"I want to make sure you're strong enough to handle this Initiation," I said, ignoring the burning in my lungs.

"Are you?" she countered.

"I know what The Order of the Silver Ghost is all about. I don't think you do. You have no idea what's in store for us."

"I didn't come here thinking this was going to be some fairy tale. I sure as hell am not getting a

Prince Charming, and I know it's going to be ugly and hard. But my eye is on the prize, and I have no doubt I'm strong enough to do whatever it takes."

"Why would you even put yourself through all this?" I asked as my legs seemed to wobble beneath me.

"Why would you?" she countered again.

"I have my reasons," I said, not wanting to discuss my family or my sister. It was none of her business really, and her knowing had no importance on whether we passed the Trials or not.

"I have my reasons as well," she mimicked.

The towering oak trees on each side of us caused a pattern of shade then sunlight, shade then sunlight, in a nauseating repetition that forced me to stop running in order to not vomit. Portia continued to jog in place as I bent over and braced my hands on the tops of my knees. I knew she had to be loving every moment of my misery, but I couldn't focus on her right now because that would have required me lifting my head enough to look at her, which wasn't an option.

"Do you plan on being drunk at every Trial?" she asked.

"I plan on doing whatever the fuck I want," I snapped, not appreciating her passive-aggressive judgment.

"Yeah," she said as she spun on her heels. "I

already figured that out about you." She continued on with her jog, not caring if I ran with her or not.

I walked over to a large oak tree and sat down against the trunk. What I really needed was a Bloody Mary to take the edge off, but I didn't see that in the immediate future. Although once we went back to the house for breakfast, I was pretty sure I could convince Mrs. H to make me one... or not. I wasn't exactly on her "good boy" list as of late. She had told me countless times that I had a bad attitude...

And she was right.

I watched Portia reach the end of the long road, turn around, and start her jog back toward me. Her body moved effortlessly, but her facial expression appeared tense and even... sad. There was more to this Barbie than I wanted to give her credit for.

She wasn't weak. I had to give her that much.

She didn't bow down to me like I had hoped she would, and in fact, I had a feeling she was going to drive me fucking crazy.

I couldn't read her. I couldn't put my finger on the exact reason why I chose her, and why I actually felt she would be able to handle each and every Trial that got thrown our way.

I would be lying if I didn't admit how hot the sex was last night. Well, except for the creepy-ass old men lined up watching us. But regardless of the situation, she lit my body on fire. As far as fuck partners went, I would say I chose wisely. But other than that... I couldn't say much more. We had a long, long road ahead of us, and I wasn't sure if the two of us could do what it took.

"You want me to go get a staff member to carry you back?" she asked as she approached and jogged in place in front of me again. Her bare shoulders glistened but she barely sweat. The Georgian heat wasn't bad, and the humidity was low since it was January, but still... "You could lean on me if you need to."

I bit my tongue because the things I wanted to say were not appropriate to say to a lady, and I still was a gentleman... sort of.

Rolling my eyes, I stood up and started to run back toward the manor without saying another word. Luckily, I was able to make it back, and couldn't have been happier when the smell of eggs and bacon met us at the door. Mrs. H had remembered my favorite breakfast, and right now, the grease was extremely needed for my abused body.

"Oh, laddie," she said as she exited the kitchen, surprised to see both Portia and me enter the house. "I wasn't sure where you both had gone, so I put your breakfast on trays and had them brought to your room. They should still be warm."

"Thank you, Mrs. H," I said, trying not to sound like I was in the middle of an asthma attack.

"Yes, thank you, Mrs. Hawthorne," Portia said, not sounding like she had gone on a run at all.

When we entered the bedroom, my mouth watered for the food. I saw a large box on the bed, but really didn't care what was in it at the moment. I had one focus only.

Bacon.

Portia, however, looked at the box, ignoring the food. "What's inside?" she asked.

I smiled as I bit into my food. Montgomery told me what the first night would most likely consist of. "That, my dear, is going to be your outfit for the night. I just have to decide what color will look best on you."

6

PORTIA

Sully wouldn't show me what was in the box, not until right before the "event". He just smirked at me every time I asked what it was, or he physically moved between us when I tried to grab for the box myself.

He even took it with him into the bathroom as he took a shower to get prepared for the evening, leaving me to stew and wonder what the hell I was going to be in for tonight.

The first Initiation night hadn't been that bad —just a bit of voyeurism with everyone watching Sully and me have sex. Maybe a naïve part of me thought that's all that would ever be asked of us. That maybe the older guys in cloaks just got off on watching.

But whatever was in that box, my instincts told

me that tonight would be... more. But *more*, *what*? How?

I was usually confident and took a no-nonsense, get-things-done approach to life. You couldn't sit there and whine about how the people around you had it better. We were all given the life we were born with, good or bad. You get what you get and you don't throw a fit, as I was told repeatedly in kindergarten.

Then you did the best you could to be happy and take care of the ones you loved the best you could. That was the only nugget of great wisdom I'd managed to gain in my twenty-three years on this earth.

Tonight would just be like any other night. I'd survive like I had the past few years since Mama had died. None of that had been easy, either. But I hadn't met a challenge yet I couldn't overcome.

So, I sat primly on the bed with my hands crossed in my lap, trying to channel my best Queen of England impression as I waited, calm and collected, slightly bored, for Sully to come out and finally reveal what was in the box.

Sully's voice boomed out at the same time he slammed open the bathroom door. "Your turn, sweet 'ems."

I swung my head towards his voice and that's when I saw it.

He had the box under his arm, but he was holding out a single blood-red leather collar.

Like a collar for a dog.

What. The. Actual. F—

"What?" Sully smirked. "Don't tell me red clashes with your baby pink nail polish."

"What the hell is that?" I bit out.

"Didn't you read the handbook?" Sully *tut tut tutted* at me.

Handbook? There was a freaking handbook? How come no one had given me a copy?

"It's men's choice. I get to choose whether to put my pet in a black, white, or red collar." His grin spread wider on his face. "The red one means I like to share."

My mouth dropped all the way open. Did that mean he—

Of course he would. He was a drunk. Completely debauched and corrupted by the wealth and privilege that had been at his beck and call since he was a kid.

He hung the red collar off his pointer finger, extending it my direction. "Chop chop. They'll be waiting on us."

My entire face and neck heated with fury. Did he really have the gall to— "You took a forty-five-minute shower and now you're telling me to rush? You can shove that collar up your ass!"

"Ah ah ah, sweet 'ems. I thought you were a good little whore. Aren't your kind supposed to spread your legs and do anything at all for a quick buck?"

Or I could wrap that collar around *his* neck and... But they probably wouldn't give me what I'd asked for if I murdered their precious Initiate, huh?

Instead, I tilted my head with a saccharine-sweet smile. "Let me guess? Daddy issues? You don't feel man enough to handle me all by yourself."

I breezed over to him and snatched the collar out of his hand.

"Fine with me if your little pecker needs a break. I understand. With all the drinking you do, it's a wonder you've managed to get it up at all."

Sully didn't say anything, but I swear I could feel the steam of rage wafting off him in my direction.

I lifted my hair and buckled the red leather around my neck. At least the leather was soft. But dear God, I had a dog collar around my neck!

If Mama could see me now...

I'd gone to Sunday School almost every week of my life up until a few years ago. Nice girls who helped organize church potlucks did not wear sex collars.

My fingers fluttered over the collar as I looked

back towards Sully. "Where's the rest of it? Or am I just supposed to wear the skimpiest underthings in the dresser?"

I walked over towards the antique dresser nestled in the corner of the large room, but Sully's unkind laugh had me stopping in my tracks.

"Oh, there's a dress code all right." His smile unnerved me. "You're looking at it." He pointed to the collar. "That and nothing else."

I felt my face go pale but wasn't going to give him the satisfaction of a reaction.

Of course I'd be naked with only the sex collar on. Silly me. What else did I expect?

Sully was enjoying this far too much, so without waiting another moment, I yanked off my soft cotton t-shirt, bra, jeans, underwear and socks. I let them fall to my feet in defiance.

I didn't think I could have done it in front of any other man. But Sully was different. He was annoying and infuriating and obviously had no respect for me. I didn't care what he thought. In fact, no one's opinion in this entire place mattered one iota in the scheme of things.

So, I stood naked except for the collar and refused to hang my head, be embarrassed, or feel shame. Sunday School be damned. Those pious bastards at church never once reached out to help me or my family in our time of need no matter how many times the pastor preached that it was the church's mission to care for the poor and down-trodden. I eventually got so disgusted by the hypocrisy I quit going.

Screw it. I didn't owe anyone anything except my family. They needed me. And no matter how Sully tried to shame me, I wouldn't let it touch me. I didn't know how many times I'd have to repeat it to myself, but I whispered it internally at least one more time before Sully and I headed downstairs:

For my family, I would do anything.

Absolutely *anything*.

I braced myself.

I prepared mentally.

At least I thought I had.

But the sheer amount of flesh that hit my eyes all at once when we got to the bottom of the stairs...

I'd never seen so many naked people. Sprawled on sumptuous settees. Arched over armchairs. Buttocks up on special benches that seemed both created for the occasion and yet also antique? How long had people been up to this kinky stuff I'd never even *known about*?

I blinked in shock.

"Close your mouth, baby bird. It's not like you're a virgin," Sully whispered in my ear.

I slammed my mouth closed at that and glared at him. Of course not, I hadn't been a virgin. But still, before all this, I'd barely ever seen *anyone* naked. The few boyfriends I'd had—well, we'd never exactly done it with the lights *on*, ya know.

Most of the guys I'd dated also lived with their families. We were all dirt poor so we took it where we could get it. Back seats of cars usually. Sometimes in a back shed. Up in one guy's fairly sturdy treehouse that had been in his parents' backyard since he was a kid. And yes, it was weird looking at the crayon stick drawings of his family tacked to the wall as he drilled in and out of me.

But still, none of that could have prepared me for *this*.

The white ballroom was packed, but instead of the floor being empty like it had been for the Initiation ceremony, it was full of furniture. Even more furniture than I'd seen at first glance.

Men lounged in daybeds, cloaks unfurled all around them as beautiful young women bobbed up and down between their legs.

Over in the corner, another woman was tied to a large wooden X, where three men took turns flogging her. She squirmed and screamed out in ecstasy for *"more!"*.

While I was still taking it all in, a man approached. He was older, skinnyish, but he had multiple folds of pale skin hanging from his chin like a turtle come out of its shell. He didn't bother with any niceties. His beady blue eyes were only on me. Actually, his beady blue eyes were only on my *body*. I don't think his gaze ever lifted north of my chest.

He didn't even introduce himself. He just immediately reached out and grabbed my nipple, squeezing and twisting hard.

I slapped him and yanked away.

All movement in the room stopped.

Oh shit.

That was bad.

I hadn't meant to do it. It was just an impulse. Anything to get the slimy old man's hands off me. But by the sour expressions on the faces all around me, I'd apparently committed a big secret society faux pas.

Turtle Neck turned angry eyes on Sully. "Care to explain the disrespectful actions of your pet? If it can't mind its elders, you shouldn't bring it out in public."

It?

Okay, I'd expected some misogyny, but this bastard took the cake. He was obviously only in the Order because no woman in her right mind would ever fuck him without being heavily incentivized to.

I looked up to Sully, expecting... I didn't know what I was expecting.

But it wasn't the carefully carved expression of amusement on his features. It wasn't like when we were alone together in the bedroom and he gave me shit. I'd swear there was an angry intensity underneath the casual amiability he was putting on.

He slapped the man on the shoulder who'd just assaulted me. "Of course, George. But those cataracts of yours must be acting up again. Because if you lean in and look closely, you'll see she's wearing a red collar, not white. She's mine to share with whom *I* wish. She's not a free-for-all buffet. And I've decided *not* to give you permission to touch my lovely jewel tonight."

With that, Sully himself reached out and grasped my breast, massaging it in front of the gathered crowd. But unlike gross Turtle Neck, he was gentle. At first anyway. After only a few moments, though, he plucked at my nipple.

Unlike the other man's touch, Sully knew exactly how to play me. A spasm rocked me as he tweaked me like he was tuning a guitar. The men around us laughed and Sully smiled triumphantly.

"When they're feral like this one is," he said loudly, "sometimes it takes a master's touch."

I wanted to roll my eyes. Master's touch my ass.

Turtle Neck wasn't happy with Sully's explanation either, apparently. He licked his top lip with a sloppy, slug-like tongue. "Give her to me. Four hours in my cage and she'll be singing a different tune. I know her kind. She'll break in no time."

Sully met the man's eyes, and I wasn't sure, but I would've sworn a silent battle passed between them. In the end, Sully smiled, wrapped an arm around my bare shoulder, and gave a polite shrug before leading me away without a word—something I didn't know he was capable of.

I wasn't sure where he was taking me, but I was happy to follow. Anything to be away from that group of men who'd smiled and approved of Turtle Neck's words and actions.

Sully leaned over and whispered in my ear, "He was out of line. But you do deserve to be punished for that little stunt."

"What?" I hissed, looking up at Sully. It had felt like he was on my side.

All of a sudden, he sat down on a leather bench, using the momentum to swing me down over and across his lap.

I was still trying to orient myself and sit up

when an explosion of fire lit across my ass. His hand. My ass.

Sully had just *spanked* me. I yelped and tried to spin in his lap, but his other arm was a firm bar across my back.

He spanked me in quick succession *ten* more times. Each swat had more power and more sting than the one before it. I'd never in my life been spanked before. Dad was an asshole, but we weren't that kind of family.

And here I was now, a twenty-three-year-old woman, getting *spanked.* I didn't want to whimper or cry out, but damn if Sully wasn't making it impossible. It hurt. It fucking hurt! Not to mention the humiliation of being bent over a man's knee completely naked with an upturned ass on full display...

Then, as quickly as it had begun, it was over. Except that my backside was still on fire from the contact. Clapping came from behind us. Was he just showing off for those ignorant bastards back there?

But I barely had time to react to one thing before Sully was waving someone over towards us. Sully readjusted us on the bench as the man approached, swinging me back around—his strength so infuriating, I was just a mere puppet in his hands—so that I was seated on the bench. I'd barely gotten my seat, and good God, *ow*, my back-side was still *smarting*.

I barely got a glimpse of the guy approaching. Just enough to tell he was tall, lean, with a handsome, slightly weathered face. Dark hair going silver at the sides. He looked like a late 1990s Richard Gere.

Oh, and there was the fact that he was totally naked except for some tight silky boxer briefs.

"Behind her," Sully commanded as soon as he reached us.

The man obeyed, slinging one leg over the bench.

"Closer," Sully barked.

I felt the heat of the Richard Gere lookalike at my back.

I wasn't sure how I felt about all this, but then again, this new guy wasn't repulsive or taking any liberties. My heart rate still sped up. Everything tonight was happening so quickly I didn't have time to figure out how I felt about one thing before we were on to the next. Maybe that was the point? Maybe if I just let go of my usually iron control and... dear God, maybe if I just let go and trusted Sully, I could get through this.

Sully certainly seemed calm and in control. He was keeping the Richard Gere lookalike in line. The man was only doing exactly what Sully said. And somehow knowing Sully was in charge —in spite of how much I despised him —relaxed me.

At least he had never referred to me as *it*, and when he'd called me a pet earlier in the room, I had the feeling it was more to get under my skin than anything he really believed.

Still, I wasn't about to let down my guard. This was just another in a long list of experiences in my life I just had to survive.

"Reach around and fondle her breasts."

Hands extended from behind me and the man lifted my breasts experimentally in his hands, as if testing the weight. Then he began to massage circles with his fingers, teasing my nipple with light flicks of his thumb.

"That's riiiight," Sully breathed out. "Just like that."

There was something in Sully's voice—a heat that hadn't been there before. He was— I swallowed hard as my nipples were pinched between thumb and forefinger. Sully's eyes blazed into mine the whole time.

They weren't his hands, but because it was his intention, moving and caressing at each of his instructions, they almost felt like they were.

And then Sully reached forward and ran his own hands up my inner thighs. Four hands on me, all seeking my pleasure. I'd never—This wasn't anything like I'd expected—

Sully's expression eased into a lazy smile when he felt my slickness there.

I couldn't help it. I was on a roller-coaster ride of sensation. From fury to embarrassment to getting ridiculously turned on by Sully commanding another man to touch my body. And now... now him adding his own hands. I shuddered and relaxed more deeply into their touch.

Sully shifted so his entire body was closer. He was still in his fine tux, completely dressed. But the way he slid his hands up and down my thighs, ghosting ever closer to my center—

I gasped out and arched my back in pleasure once Sully finally whispered his thumb against my clit, just the barest touch.

Sully's voice was thick as he gave his next instruction. "Lift her hair and suck on the back of her neck right below her earlobe."

My breath hitched in a swallow I couldn't quite manage. Soon heated lips were on the back of my neck, eagerly following Sully's commands. The rest of the room's activity and noise had begun to drop away.

There was just Sully, leaning over me, his after-shave intoxicating. "You like that, don't you? Not too bad to be shared after all, huh?"

"Shut up and don't ruin it," I gasped, reaching for him.

But he pulled away before I could even grab for his shirt. "Don't forget who's in control here. Tonight and always."

Then he reached between my legs and further, pinching my still-sore ass.

I winced but with his other hand, he'd finally committed to stroking my clit. The fireworks were beginning to pop off uncontrollably throughout my body, radiating outward from my center.

But I also felt panicked.

Everything was so out of control.

This wasn't who I was.

I made the rules.

I made charts and calendars and organized every day down to the minute sometimes. I made schedules and paid bills and took people to doctor appointments and the clinic. I budgeted our meager earnings into envelopes every month, cut out coupons, did side jobs, everything I could think of to hold body and soul together for my family.

But here, in this moment, I was completely stripped down. There was a cool leather bench underneath me. The hot smell of sweat, sex, and aftershave thick in the air. Two sets of strong male hands on my body. Sully's voice in my ear, a roar compared to the pleasured groans and occasionally faked noises of female ecstasy echoing around the room.

Then Sully shocked me even further, slipping one of his thick fingers into my wet, sopping pussy just long enough to gather some cream and bring it to my lips.

"Open up and taste how sweet," he commanded.

I looked up helplessly into his devil's eyes and I opened up. He wasn't gentle as he shoved his finger coated in my essence inside, but I didn't miss how his own nostrils flared at the action.

I got it, then. None of my usual coping tools were available to me.

I couldn't take control or make an Excel spreadsheet for this.

Sully knew it, too. But for as much of a layabout as he seemed the rest of the time, here, in this moment, he was completely in his element.

His eyes blazed with fire as his gaze seared into mine. Our eyes stayed locked as he ordered, "Eat her out while I fuck her mouth."

Immediately the heat disappeared from behind me. But Sully didn't even let me look at the other man. He immediately slid in front of me, laying me back on the bench. Then he kicked off his suit pants and straddled my face.

His long, intimidating cock hung heavy in front

of my lips, bobbing there angry and red and bulging.

"Take it in your hands and suck it like you want to vacuum every drop of cum out of my balls. Like you can't get enough of it. My cum is everything you've ever wanted in the world, the only thing you've ever fucking wanted."

I spasmed, almost coming on the spot from his words alone. Because yes, it was the only thing I'd ever wanted, the only thing I'd ever fucking wanted, how did the fucker, how did he—

He grabbed his cock and pushed it towards my lips.

"Show me how much you want whatever it is you came here for. Convince me you want it."

His rough, masculine voice growling such dirty commands made my brain short-circuit. I don't know how else to describe why I did what I did next.

"Now. Eat her out like a fucking feast."

I didn't realize the words weren't directed at me until a hot, wet mouth latched onto my clit.

My mouth opened in an O of surprise and Sully took the opportunity to feed his cock between my lips.

For a second, the out-of-control feeling threatened to make me panic, scream, and flail. Fight or flight. I couldn't do this. I was out, I couldn't—

"Shh, that's right. Take what I'm giving. No thinking. Give up thinking and just do. Suck my cock and embrace being the dirty little whore you are."

I cried out, the emotions and physical sensations too overwhelming—but...

Then I gave in.

I surrendered.

I opened up and took Sully's huge cock as deep as I could, grabbing on to the thick base if only for something to ground me and tether me to reality.

His masculine growl of pleasure at the action removed my last bits of sanity.

Suddenly everything that had seemed so complicated only moments ago, became easy. Clear. So simple.

Suck Sully's cock.

Suck Sully's cock like it was the only thing in this entire world. In this moment, it was. And it was so perfect in this moment, my life calmed down to this one object, worshipping him, bringing him pleasure, driving him insane, making him explode.

Make him growl like that again. Blow his mind. Suck the cum out of him until he felt what he was making me feel.

Because as the mouth worked my clit—which in my misting-over brain felt like just another extension of Sully—pleasure lit up and down every nerve in my entire body.

"That's right." Sully's voice came out strangled.

I was affecting him and that made me burn hotter than any touch on my body.

I closed my lips even tighter around his cock, pressing as hard as I could on the shaft with my lips and then slowing down as I hit the crown. I moved tortuously slow as I bobbed on the bulbous tip. I sucked as hard as I could, trying to give as much pressure as possible while I bobbed back and forth a few quick times before plunging him deep into my throat again. He'd driven me out of my mind. I was a mindless creature, and I would make him the same.

He swore and his hand dropped to tangle in my hair.

He reached back and swatted my breast as he bucked into my mouth, down my throat. "Fuck," he muttered. "Just like that. Fuck. Keep doing that. Now grab my balls."

I did. They felt full to bursting, straining against the sack. I cupped them and lifted them up and against his body, determined to milk him hard.

Pleasing him was a clear, easy task. The easiest thing I'd done in months, in years, and suddenly I wanted it more than anything.

My own orgasm flowed over me like a wave

lighting my skin from within. Tears coursed down my cheeks as I hummed and howled and moaned on Sully's cock, shuddering around him.

And then, with a roar that drowned out all the other activity in the room, Sully shoved deep as deep could go into my throat, the salt of his seed spilling down.

So much of it that it filled up my throat, my mouth, and dripped out the corners of my lips.

Sully didn't remove his cock. He bobbed in and out, looking down at me with surprised, heated eyes. He liked the sight of his cock spilling semen out of my mouth and down my neck onto my breasts.

I felt like we stayed like that for half an hour, but it was probably only minutes. Sully finally pulled back, lifting his leg from where he straddled above me. I wondered if that was it. Was the Trial over?

The rest of the members seemed too preoccupied with their own dicks to pay any more attention to us. It was just the two of us in this little corner of the room. I didn't know where the other man had gone, and I didn't care.

Sully didn't say a word. He just reached out, rubbed some still shining cum from my bottom lip and spread it all around my chest and breasts.

Like he was marking me as his own.

I'd never experienced anything like this: extreme intensity followed by the most boring doldrums possible.

Half a week later after the most mind-blowing sexual experience of my life and I was ready to go stir-crazy. It didn't help that my supposed "partner" in all this had decided to disappear into the business end of a bottle.

Or I should say, bottle after bottle.

I don't think he'd been fully sober *once* ever since that night with the collar and what we'd done downstairs... I reached my hands to my heated cheeks. Anyway, he'd been checked out ever since.

Sometimes he wouldn't even leave the room for meals, so *I* was locked in here with him, too.

Because the Almighty Handbook said women weren't allowed to leave their room without their Initiate by their side as escort. Some sexist bullshit was what it was. I was a prisoner unless Sully agreed to even take me outside. Even *dogs* got walked!

And I swore, if I had to look at these four walls anymore, I was going to scream.

I'd been nice. I'd given him space to work out... well, whatever it was rich, privileged boys like him needed to work out. But enough was enough. I was like a plant. I needed plenty of sunlight and vitamin D to thrive.

I walked over to the curtains and threw them open, flooding the room in bright, late morning light.

"Rise and shine!" I sang out cheerily.

Sully moaned and hiked his covers up over his head, burying deeper into his pillow.

I'd already cleaned up my floor pallet of pillows and blankets I slept on by the bay window, but the bed was the same disaster of sheets and blanket it always was.

He'd untucked everything the first day and refused to let Mrs. Hawthorne put it back right.

"Come on," I said impatiently. "No sleeping in for spoiled little rich boys. Chop chop! Some of us actually care about our health and staying in shape." And getting the hell out of this stuffy, suffocating room.

"Go back to bed," was all the gruff moan I got in response.

Oh my gosh, was he serious? "But it's already ten a.m. and you haven't done anything but lay there," I said indignantly. "Is this how you spend your life? Or should I say *waste* your life?" I finished in a mutter.

If I was back home, I'd already have cooked everyone breakfast, packed lunches, and had last night's laundry folded and put away.

I tried to stay up last night to keep an eye on Sully's drinking so maybe today could be different from the last few, but it was no use.

I was too used to collapsing into bed exhausted at 9:30 or 10 at the latest.

Sully had been on his fourth glass by then, though by the multiple bottles rolling around the bottom of the bed, I bet he abandoned cups and started chugging straight from the bottleneck at some point.

Was he really just a total drunk, or was he just trying to avoid actually having a real conversation with me?

Either way, something had to change. My body felt all wrong. Not having a routine was not okay for me. Some hours I'd feel tired and despondent, while other hours I'd feel jacked up with energy but without any way to expend it.

Yesterday, I'd played solitaire for hours on end —a paltry distraction because every minute of free time, all I could do was obsess about the girls back home.

Tanya could easily get overwhelmed when a lot of responsibility got put on her shoulders. I wasn't sure how much Reba would be able to help her out, and LeAnn was still just a baby. Okay, so four-teen wasn't that young. When I was that old, I was already a mini mom—or at least my mom's right-hand girl. But all of us had tried hard to protect LeAnn's childhood, so she was more a kid than any of us had ever been at her age.

When Dad was home, he'd had strict ideas about men's and women's roles, too. He made the money, and, in return, we made a nice, comfortable home for him. It was the least we could do for the audacity of all coming out female, with no strap-ping boys to carry on the family name and legacy.

Ha. What a legacy. When the going got tough, apparently "real men" just checked the eff out.

I looked back at Sully in disgust. How many nights had I seen my father like this? A man who could have been so much more—but wasn't. I think I hated my father more for it. Knowing he *could* have been there if he'd put forth even an iota of his energy and the character he'd apparently lost a long time ago, back when he was the man my mother first fell in love with.

I knew men. And I was an idiot for thinking I could relax and let my guard down even the littlest bit around Sullivan VanDoren.

I steeled myself, grabbed the top of his blanket, and yanked. The entire blanket came away in my arms, much to my delight.

There. Take *that.*

"What the fuck?" Sully yelled, holding up a hand against the bright yellow light of the day. "Give that the fuck back or you'll be sorry."

I scampered backwards and as I did, tripped a little and stumbled to the floor. Where I suddenly got a good look under the bed. My eyes widened when I saw a box in the back corner. A crate full of more booze.

At nighttime when I made my pallet on the floor, it was always pitch black under the bed, but with the room currently flooded with light, I could see everything. There was one box with a fancy bourbon label and beside it, a couple other fancy bottles of whiskey and vodka.

"Son of a—" I let go of Sully's blanket, which he immediately snatched back from the floor. The bed squeaked above me, and I imagined him turning around and settling back in. His snores returned almost immediately.

Which absolutely infuriated me.

He thought he got to cruise through these months in an alcoholic haze while I was stuck being stone cold sober?

No damn way, buddy.

Once his snores became even more sonorous and deep, I squeezed my thin frame underneath the bed just enough to get a handle on the box of booze. Wedging one foot against a wall, I managed to pull it out even though it was damn heavy, and the bottles clanked against one another loudly.

I thought for sure Sully would wake up, but his snores went on.

I fought a maniacal giggle.

After I got the big crate out, I went back for the last few separate bottles. Then I got everything arranged and shoved open the window.

When it was all perfect, I hollered at the top of my lungs, "Sully! Wake up or I'm dumping it all!"

Sully jumped at my shrill tone and his half-lidded eyes opened, wincing against the light. He was about to turn over again and keep ignoring me, but I clanked two of the bottles together loudly.

It was obviously a sound he was very familiar with, because finally, I had his attention. He pushed down the blanket and sat up, looking adorably befuddled, and also unfortunately terribly sexy with the several days' dark scruff he was sporting.

He is not sexy, he is the enemy, I tried to scold myself, but his angry growl had my thoughts quickly clearing.

"What the hell do you think you're doing?"

I looked down to where I had the big box of bottles resting precariously on the open window ledge. I'd neatly laid the free-standing bottles on top.

"I think we should make a new rule. No drinking allowed."

Sully sat up, his eyes suddenly much clearer. Clear and dark and angry. A tingle raced up my spine. I smiled and held up one of the free bottles. I'd already pulled out the stopper, and I tipped it upside down.

Crystal-like amber liquid flowed from the bottle down onto the green grass below. It was quite a beautiful display in the golden sunlight of mid-morning.

"Stop it!" Sully's face went panicked, and he held out his hand like that would make the whiskey pause mid-flow.

"Are you ready to negotiate?"

But Sully's eyes only went darker. "I don't negotiate with terrorists."

I shrugged. "Fine with me. I never thought booze should be allowed in our room in the first place anyway."

And with that, I took a quick glance below to make sure no gardeners or anyone else happened to be passing by, then I nudged the entire box out the window, tossing the last two bottles after it for good measure.

It exploded on the lawn below in a fantastic burst of glass, liquid, and wood. I grinned, feeling extremely satisfied with myself.

Extremely satisfied, that was, until I glanced back and saw Sully's dark, furious face.

"You're going to regret that, little girl."

S trangle or fuck.

I was going to do one or the other to this woman before me.

"Have you lost your mind?" I seethed, standing up from the bed completely naked and not giving a shit that my dick was on full display. "Do you have any idea how much money you just threw out the window?"

She shrugged as if she hadn't done anything worth mentioning. "I'm sure it's nothing you can't handle, Mr. Rich Boy." She walked past me and didn't seem to flinch at my anger or my nudity. "Maybe now, you can do more than just drink your hours away."

"First of all, princess," I said as I casually leaned against the bottom bedpost and crossed my arms against my chest. "There is plenty of booze in this manor. I'm not worried about going dry." I was pissed, but I wasn't going to let on exactly how much. I didn't want her to know that her little stunt had gotten my blood boiling. I needed to remain cool and collected.

She took a deep breath, and I watched her shoulders rise and fall. She didn't say anything with her mouth, but her eyes said enough.

"Fuck you, bastard."

"I've tried to play nice," I said, taking a step toward her.

She laughed. "Nice? Is this what you call nice?" She laughed again. "I'm curious what your asshole looks like then."

"You haven't seen the worst of me, or this place yet. Trust me on that."

"Frankly," she began as she placed her hands on her hips. "I would take anything over what I've seen. You're pathetic."

"You just don't know when you should shut those pretty little lips of yours." I took another step toward her. "And it's also time we have a little talk about the rules around here. You're in my world now. Mine. So, clearly we need a little educating."

"Stop," she said as she took a step back toward the chairs in front of the fireplace. "Don't come any closer." She glanced down at my dick. "And put some clothes on."

"When are you going to understand that you don't get to be the one who issues the demands here? You aren't in control, sweet 'ems." I closed the distance between us, grabbed her by the arm, and yanked her to the bed. Tossing her onto the mattress, I straddled her, taking her wrists and lifting them above her head.

She bucked and squealed against me, but my weight made her attempt of escape futile.

"Get off of me," she shouted, tossing her head side to side and writhing beneath me.

"Or what?"

I liked showing her that she had no power in this situation. She could do absolutely nothing to fight me off, and she was not the one in control.

I was.

"I think it's time I teach you a lesson. A real lesson. You aren't the one with the power here. Not even a little bit." Gripping her wrists with just one hand, I used my other to start lowering her pants.

Why should *I* be the only one naked?

"What are you doing? Stop it!" She tried to wiggle free, and although she was quite strong, I was stronger.

"It's time for some morning exercise. You're the

one who's always trying to nag me to workout with you every day... well, now I'm ready."

"Get off of me! Now!"

"Gladly," I said. "It'll make my mission even easier."

Pulling her up harshly, I tugged her pants down at the same time. The action was quick enough that Portia wasn't able to stop me from doing so. I paused just long enough to appreciate her white lace thong, but that had to go as well.

Pushing her up against the wall to help aid me in stripping her bare, I mastered her. I had to admit the little vixen winded me with her fight. But I was a man with a purpose, and that purpose was to shed her of every ounce of clothing she had on.

"You can't do this!" she screeched when I finally got her bra free and tossed it to the ground.

"It appears that I can," I said, slightly breathless from the exertion.

"This isn't a Trial. I don't have to fuck you. We aren't under the watch of the Elders. This room is off limits! I'm saying no, and—"

"I'm not asking," I growled when she was finally naked and restrained. I had her hands held above her head again, and I pressed my hard cock against the smoothness of her skin.

God, I wanted to fuck her. But I had other things in mind.

"You're a brat, Portia Collins. And I'm about to teach you what happens to girls like you. You're playing in the big leagues now, and you'll soon see I'm not a man to mess with."

She raised her knee, but luckily missed my balls which I knew were her intended target. Spreading her legs and nestling in between her thighs, I then pressed my full weight against her. I squeezed a little tighter on her wrists, lowered my lips to her neck and bit. Deciding that nothing would be better than marking her flawless skin, I began to nibble, lick and suck, visibly claiming her as mine.

"You're a drunken ass," she said, although her struggles ceased when the biting began.

"And you're an annoying gold digger. So, we both shall wear our badges of honor." I continued to mark her neck, liking the idea that every time she looked at herself in the mirror, she would see a part of me left behind.

"I'm far from a gold digger," she said.

I pulled away and looked her straight in the eyes. "I'm ashamed of you, princess. I didn't figure you for a liar." Her lips were so close a strong urge to kiss them washed over me. I quickly shook it off and chalked it up to momentary insanity.

"I'm not a liar," she spat. "You know nothing about me."

"And you know nothing about me," I countered. "And yet, you feel you can stand there with your tiara and cast judgment on me every single hour of every single day. And you actually blame me for wanting to drink my misery away?"

"Fine," she snapped. "Let go of me, and I'll leave you alone from this point on. You stay in your corner of the room, and I'll stay in mine."

I chuckled. "Too late. You crossed the line of no return. I told you that you'd regret what you did, and I mean what I say. I don't make idle threats."

"I'll scream," she threatened.

With a smile, I said, "Oh, I hope you do."

I brought my hand down to her pussy and cupped her heat in my palm. She gasped, and her eyelids fluttered which had my cock twitching in anticipation for more.

"When you resisted a member of the Order the other night, you could have really fucked things up for the both of us. If he was an Elder, or wanted to make more of an issue, you and I could have been forced to face whatever consequences they came up with, or even risked failing the Initiation all together. I don't know about you, sugar, but I'm not in this for my health. This hellhole isn't exactly my idea of paradise. We're here for an end goal, and your bratty self is not going to ruin it."

Slapping her pussy, I then thrust my finger

inside of her, pumping it slow and steady. She cried out but didn't fight off the intrusion in any way.

Releasing her wrists from above her head, I used my now free hand to caress her breast as I finger fucked her into submission. I could still see the fire in her eyes, but she no longer attempted to fight me off.

"You're wet," I said, loving how quickly her body responded to my touch. "Dripping."

She didn't reply but closed her eyes and parted her lips instead. Her pussy clenched around my finger as her breathing sped up.

"Do you want to cum on my hand, princess? Coat my finger with your cream?"

Her gasps of air turned to soft moans, and she began to meet my finger pumping with her own gyrating. I added a second finger and stopped moving my hand. I scissored them, spreading her hole as I coated them with her intense arousal. Pulling out of her, I chuckled as she moaned out in disappointment.

"Don't stop," she whispered. "Keep going."

Flipping her around so her breasts were up against the wall, I slapped her ass hard. "You aren't in control, Portia. You don't get to tell me what to do. It's that attitude that will get you in trouble and force me to clean up your mess." I took hold of her hair and yanked her head back. "Put your hands on the wall."

She did as I commanded without hesitation. Still holding her hair, I spanked her again, and again, loving how she remained in position the entire time.

I didn't mind the fight, but I fucking loved the surrender.

Taking advantage of the fact that my fingers were still coated with her juices, I brought them to her anus and pressed hard. I didn't breach fully, but definitely made my presence there noticeable. Portia tensed, but still didn't break her position.

I tugged on her hair as I inserted one finger even further into her ass. She whimpered but didn't fight. Inch by inch, I eased my finger in until I was firmly rooted in her ass.

"Time for us to go on our morning walk," I said as I released her hair.

All I would need to leash my pet was my finger hooked inside of her tight little asshole.

"Sully..." she gasped out.

"Let's walk over to the window and see the damage you caused." I pushed her forward with my hand, driving my finger even deeper inside of her tight asshole. I kept it angled like a hook so I had full control of her body.

Portia gingerly began to walk, raising on her

tiptoes when the movement caused my finger to go even deeper inside of her ass. She didn't stop, however, but continued toward the window.

"That's right. Keep walking," I praised, enjoying how her ass cheeks caressed my wrist with her slow stride. "Let's go see what your naughty ass did to the grounds of the Oleander. I'm sure the staff are going to love you."

"I'm sorry," she said as I pressed her up against the glass of the window to look down. "I hadn't intended on forcing someone else to clean up the mess."

"Maybe I should force you to clean it up with my finger still planted inside your ass," I suggested.

She tensed but didn't say a single word.

Pulling my finger out, only to shove it back in, I began finger fucking her ass. She mewled in such a way I considered shoving my cock where my finger was, but I needed to stay focused on what my intention of this morning was all about.

Portia Collins needed to release the control.

"Let's go over some rules," I began. "First rule is I don't do mornings. But if you let me fucking sleep to a normal hour, and stop flitting about making noise before the sun is even fully out, I'll make a promise to get up and take you on your run. Second rule is you are going to stop sleeping on the damn floor. I may be an asshole, but the

Southern gentleman inbred in me hates it. You'll sleep in the bed with me regardless of how you feel about it. And third rule is you stop fighting me on every single thing. I know this world. I fucking hate it, but I understand it. You don't. You're going to have to trust me. So, when I tell you to jump, you simply ask how high. Are we clear on the rules?"

She nodded as she placed her palms on the window to help steady her stance as my finger assaulted her tight little hole.

As I continued to finger fuck her ass, I leaned toward her ear and said, "The only way we're going to survive this place is by you playing the part of the good little belle. You may not like it, but you don't call the shots here." I added a second finger to join the first which had her crying out. "Are we clear?"

"Yes. Yes." She nodded as her breathing came out in tiny huffs.

"The next time you try to test my patience or push me for a fight, it won't be my finger in your ass but something much, much larger. Are we clear?"

She nodded again, but I wasn't satisfied with that as the answer. I pumped my fingers even deeper.

"Yes," she squealed, raising up on her toes as

she answered. "I'll be the perfect little belle from now on."

"Within these walls, the men are in control. It's the way it is. Is it fucked up? Yes. But it's the way it has always been and thinking your perky blonde ass can change that fact is foolish." I pulled out my fingers slowly, but then shoved them back in with effortless speed.

"Ahh," she half moaned, half cried. "It stings! It's too much. You're stretching me too much."

"Good. Maybe you'll remember this next time you think you call the shots." I continued to double digit fuck her ass, taking a perverse sense of enjoyment at the sounds of her whimpers and moans. "So, answer me again. Who's in control in this manor?"

"The men are," she answered softly and obediently.

"Good girl," I said, pulling my fingers out of her ass.

Fighting the urge to bend her over the bed and fuck her, I decided the punishment would be more effective if I left her wanting for more. She didn't get to cum, and that need would hopefully drive her mad. Using all the willpower I had in my body, I walked to the bathroom, closed the door behind me, and turned on the shower.

On cold.

S hit, they'd all be on my tail any minute. I had to work fast.

Or rather, *run*. I had to *run fast*. Faster than I ever had in my whole life.

Because you see, another invitation had come during dinner. Sully's face had gone pale as soon as he read it, which I didn't take as a good sign.

"Fox hunt," was all he'd been able to utter before I grabbed the invitation from his hand, along with the sizeable white box that had arrived with the invitation.

Inside had been a leather cloak that smelled a hundred years old with a glassy-eyed stuffed fox head attached to the hood.

Oh, but that wasn't all that was in the box. Of course it wasn't. Not with these sadistic bastards.

There was also a plush fluffy little red fox tail—attached to the end of a buttplug.

At least *that* looked new, still was in the packaging. But what the hell?

"They can't really mean for me to—" I started, only to meet Sully's dead-serious gaze.

"That's exactly what they intend."

We had a couple of hours to wait before the actual Fox Hunt began. Or rather, the Human Hunt. Hadn't I read a story about this once in Jr. High? *The Most Dangerous Game*? This sort of shit was supposed to be outlawed.

You couldn't hunt people for sport!

But now, as I fled through the underbrush, sticking close to the tree line, I had to admit it appeared I was wrong. Even as I ran, my anus squeezed unintentionally around the buttplug inserted securely inside me. Good God, that was the last thing I needed to be focusing on right now.

Because apparently people could and very much *did* hunt other people for sport. No matter how they tried to dress it up and tell themselves I was a dehumanized fox for the night.

The baying of hounds in the distance made goosebumps erupt all up and down my limbs. Well, even more goosebumps.

It was January, and even Georgia got freaking near-freezing temperatures in winter. I could see my breath frosting in front of my face. And apart from the hood and the buttplug, naturally there'd been nothing else in the box.

I wasn't even allowed *shoes*.

I couldn't feel my toes, and I'd only been out here twenty minutes. I'd been assured by one of the Elders with a viscous, unpleasant smile the temperature wouldn't matter when I dared ask about it. I'd be caught and blooded before the cold could do me any real damage, he'd assured me. The way he'd been twisting his hands at the time made me think he was hoping to be the fucker who did the catching.

Whatever the fuck "blooding" was. I had not been informed as to its definition, and I did not want to know. In fact, I was actively trying not to think about it.

I'd started to ask how I could "win" the game— could I outlast them until morning or—

But Sully had shaken his head at me and grabbed for my wrist in warning. And that's when I understood. This was never meant to be a fair game. There was no way for *me* to win. There was only losing for me in this game—being caught and "blooded".

The game was seeing which of the big strong men chased me down as trophy for the night.

I felt sick.

Especially now that I was out here running for my life as the baying of the dogs was followed by the long horn blast signaling that my twenty-minute head-start was over.

Shit! I was behind schedule from where I wanted to be by now.

Because I knew something those big, bad men chasing me down on horses didn't: this little fox had a few tricks up her sleeve.

I headed into the trees and yanked off the stinking cloak, supposedly a kindness to save my tender skin from the elements.

But I'd been warned. In reality, the leather had been *sprayed* for added scent, a giant neon sign to those trained hunting bloodhounds.

As if this whole thing wasn't already rigged—a multitude of Order members being on freaking *horses* with scenting hounds to help them run down a single girl, naked, barefoot in the woods.

But no, they tried to fool us "foxes" by giving us the cloak, ostensibly part of the tradition and to make us feel less naked. When really it was just a hidden ruse to be able to find us quicker because of the scent they sprayed on it without telling us.

My fury at the whole situation made my motions quicker and more focused.

I worked a small area, rubbing the cloak against every tree trunk I could.

"Ow," I hissed. *Fuck.* I'd stepped on another goddamned branch twig in the darkness, and it hurt like a *mother* on the soles of my bare feet. I was trying to step as carefully as I could, while, ya know, fleeing through the woods.

Focus. Don't get mad about what you can't control. It was the mantra of my whole life, right? I should be good at it by now. I bit my cheek against the pain in my foot and balled up the secretly-scented cloak. Then I tossed it up into the tree branches of a towering pine above me as high as I could.

It fell back on my head. I glared at it, but only for a second. Then I threw it again, with more force this time. It caught in the branches. Thank *God*. Though I doubted God had anything to do with this mess I was currently caught in.

I glanced upwards, but like I'd hoped, the cloak was lost among the darkness blanketing the branches and sprays of dark needles.

Then I ran hell-for-leather toward the lake, feeling the buttplug every second of the way. It was just impossible to sprint with a fairly large-sized buttplug shoved up your ass and *not* feel the freaking thing.

Aiming for the lake meant I was running diagonally back *toward* the direction the thunderous hooves were coming from. It was crazy. This was nuts. I was nuts. What the hell was I thinking? This was a crazy plan.

It was the only plan.

They want to *blood me*, remember?

Fuck. I squeezed around the plug in my ass and ran even faster. Thank goodness at least there were no thorns on the well-groomed lawn that extended a small bit into the surrounding forest. Meticulous landscaping for the *win.*

I focused on the path ahead. No distractions. No distractions. Dear Lord, this was my only chance. One crazy shot in a million.

I wouldn't be so completely sure of my plan if the note hadn't told me what to do.

The note... thank God for the note.

I prayed it hadn't been just another plan leading me straight to a torturous doom. Because with these sadistic motherfuckers, a girl never knew. I could only take a leap of faith.

Finally, the lake came into view in the distance. The surface reflected some twinkle of light from somewhere, maybe the house even further in the distance.

Time for that leap of faith.

Sully had been in a bad mood ever since the box arrived after dinner earlier tonight. I think we'd both been looking forward to a quiet evening in. We'd settled into something resembling a routine. After three weeks it was either that or go nuts.

And after his little, um, *lesson* the other day... well, I couldn't argue things weren't going more smoothly between us.

I let him sleep in. But that was only because I'd started sleeping in the bed just like he'd insisted. In the mornings, my eyes would still pop wide open with the dawn. Only to find a giant Southern boy wrapped around me like the snuggest blanky. I tried not to read into it too much. Likely he just had a bad habit of wrapping himself around whatever was in bed with him. After all, when I'd been sleeping on the ground, he'd made a mess of his sheets and blanket every night. So, surely it didn't mean much that now he simply wrapped himself up in... well, *me* in the middle of the night.

For such a grumpy man, he was shockingly cuddly.

Granted all the cuddling *did* usually lead to sex once his morning wood woke up enough to grind against my soft places... But that wasn't such a bad way to start the day.

As to how we spent the rest of the very long

days... Sometimes Sully still sullenly refused my gambits for his attention. But every so often I could cajole him out of his brooding moods long enough to play Monopoly or Scrabble, or even better yet, Speed Scrabble.

He was surprisingly competitive for someone so apathetic the rest of the time. Or maybe it just irked him losing to *me*. After an especially competitive game last week, he'd lifted me from the floor where we'd been playing, tossed me on the bed, because he'd "decided to show me who's the boss".

After that, it seemed every friendly game we played ended up with wrestling on the bed until Sully had claimed dominance.

And um, I had to say... It wasn't a bad way to pass the time.

All the time sex was certainly putting Sully in a better mood and I... Well, I opted not to think too much about it.

We were consenting adults, we were having fun, and if banging each other's brains out was the best way to get through these three months without killing each other... I figured, why try to fix what wasn't broken?

But the calm, not-as-caustic Sully disappeared as soon as the Fox Hunt invitation came. Sully barely spoke before he was ordering me to put in the buttplug while he showered.

"Use the lube, it'll help," was all he said flippantly over his shoulder before disappearing into the bathroom for one of his marathon showers.

It was good he took so long, though, because it took longer than I was comfortable admitting to work the little glass object with the fluffy tail up my backside. It just did *not* want to go in at first. I mean, I'd never even had any object *ever* up my bum before last week when Sully— When Sully—

Oh my God, I still could barely even think about what he'd done. Guiding me around like some sort of filthy, kinky puppet with his finger up my—

But Sully was right. The lube was a lifesaver.

It felt weird, though. Even weirder when I tried to get up and walk around. I involuntarily clutched around it, which made the furry tail swish against the backs of my thighs.

So, so weird.

After Sully's shower, I heard the blow-drier turn on in the bathroom. Well, apparently someone wanted to look *fancy* for his fox-hunting buddies, huh?

I didn't even know how to begin to prepare myself mentally for what I was about to face. I could have done with some moral support, that was for sure.

But I guessed that wasn't the kind of relationship Sully and I had. Better to be reminded of it now than to let the multiple acts of intimacy start to muddle my head. The sex we were having didn't mean shit to Sully.

I was a warm and willing body when there was no one else around. He was bored. I'd shut off his booze tab. Sex was the next best thing on the *Debauched Playboy's List of Distractions*, right?

My eyes fell to the floor.

Was I really that different from a whore after all?

Sully came out of the bathroom with a rush of steam surrounding him. He frowned when he saw me. "Why aren't you dressed?"

I laughed. Then realized he was serious. "In what? That?"

I pointed across the room at the old leather cloak with the grotesque fox head that was draped over the side of what I'd taken to calling the Costume Box. It was still sitting on the antique desk nestled against the wall by one of the huge windows.

"It's the rules." He walked over to the box, his back to me, then he brought it over to the bed and handed it to me. "This is it. You aren't allowed to wear anything other than this cloak."

I grabbed the box from him. Other than the cloak and the... uh, buttplug, it was empty.

Completely empty. "What about shoes. Surely they'll give me shoes at least."

Sully hadn't said much about what a "Fox Hunt" was—he himself didn't know much, only rumors about what he and his friends had heard whispered in the halls of the Oleander—but he knew the gist. The "belle" was released on the grounds and the Order members, on horseback, completed a traditional Southern Fox Hunt. That was all he'd known. They caught the fox and "blooded" the fox to celebrate the win.

Yeah. I hadn't known how the *fuck* to respond to that either.

Sully froze where he stood a moment, and, staring me straight in the eyes, a muscle in his jaw ticking, he said, "No. No shoes. Just what's in the box."

"So..." I said what he wouldn't. "Barefoot. Those fuckers are gonna make me run around outside essentially naked and barefoot while they chase me?"

Another jaw flex. And then, "I'll leave you to it."

With that, he grabbed the rest of his hunting finery and disappeared back to the bathroom to dress. Ridiculous really, since we saw each other naked all the time. But if he was going to exhibit some manners, I wasn't going to stop him.

I fingered the cloak, running my hand down the cracked, aged leather.

On the inside, it was nicer. It seemed like the inner silk lining had been replaced at some point in maybe the last twenty years.

Then I frowned. There was a little pocket on the inner lining, and it was slightly bulging.

I slid my hand inside and pulled out a small, cracked and crumpled piece of paper, brown around the edges.

A note.

I had to squint to make out the small script:

To the woman who wears this after me,

The leather is doused with fox scent.

Ditch it ASAP.

Get in the lake, wash.

Never stop running, dogs don't.

Good places to hide:

Ridge at SE edge property - rocky, bad scent trail

Dry goods cellar

Places foxes get caught most:

Ravine N property line - water too shallow

Old Barn by lake

Open fields

I flipped it over and on the back was a crude property map, arrows pointing at the spots mentioned on the opposite side.

It was then that the reality of what I was about to go through actually for *realsies* hit. I mean, on the one hand it was ludicrous. The note read like elaborate rules to a children's game. Good places for hide-and-seek.

Except what the invitation and Sully had failed to mention was what happened to me when I was inevitably *caught* beyond whatever the hell "blooding" was—which by the way I hoped was something ceremonial maybe involving red ribbons? And no, I wasn't examining the naivete of that particular thought too hard, just holding on to it because I really, deeply hoped it was true.

But beyond the "blooding," what happened next? Even if I was naive about what "blooding" might involve, I wasn't stupid enough to not get that the little naked fox-assed belle who got run down and pinned by the Big Man was *not* going to get her brains fucked out by Said Conquering Male With The Obviously Biggest Penis Of All His Friends.

It was obvious.

To the victor went the spoils, right?

I'd always only be an object to these men. A trophy to be won. And shared.

Sully had already shown he didn't mind sharing.

Oh God, I was going to be sick. I thought maybe things had been changing between Sully and me, but I'd always been a too-sentimental idiot.

What had happened to the woman who wrote the note?

There was nothing more about who she'd been, what had happened during her Fox Hunt, or if she'd gone on to get everything she ever wanted. Had she made it through the trials, and did the dreammakers grant her the biggest, most bestest shiniest dream life?

Whatever had happened to her, her experience with the Fox Hunt probably wasn't good if she'd felt moved to leave this warning note, hoping to prepare the next girl better...

You could say your safe word, a dangerous little voice inside me whispered. *Hightail it out of here before the insanity really began.*

My sisters would understand.

If I explained even half of what had been asked of me here, neither Reba nor Tanya would fault me for leaving.

Especially Reba. Angel-hearted Reba, always wanting the best for everyone. She was the mediator, stepping in when things got too heated between LeAnn and Tanya, the two hotheads in the family.

No one could stay mad when Reba lifted her quiet voice and asked for us to listen to one another and stop fighting. But each of my sisters had superpowers like that.

Tanya was brash and brave and outspoken and a lot of days I wished I was more like her. Reba was the peacemaker and she'd mastered being fully content with her small, repetitive little life. LeAnn was the beauty—popular, and talented, too. She was the only one of us who could actually sing, in spite of being named for country singers.

My sisters were women who were going places.

But their futures depended on me not wimping out just because I had a little... humans-wanting-to-hunt-me-for-sport problem.

I wouldn't leave them high and dry.

After all, I wasn't my father.

Now I was sprinting for the lake. I was coming around from the back side, and in the dark, no one should be able to see me.

But I was close enough that, even though I really did believe they couldn't see me and the men were just screaming out for shits and giggles—it was eerie as hell to see lights in the distance and hear voices calling out cheerily to: "Chase the bitch down! First to blood drinks free for a year!"

I almost tripped at hearing them talking about the mysterious *blood* part of this ritual but caught myself just in time. I was finally at the lake's edge. The shore was a mixture of rock, mud, and murky water.

I dropped to my knees so they wouldn't see me.

Holy f—! I mouthed, managing only at the very last moment to keep my yelp in shock at the freezing cold water on the *inside*. I bit my lip on the *f* and clamped down.

Holy Jesus the water was cold. Cold cold cold. And I was extremely naked. No wet suit in sight. Holy Jesus son of Mary and *Joseph*—

But I couldn't just hover here, half in, half out of the water.

I lowered myself the last bit into the lake water as quietly as I could. I couldn't afford any splash.

If I thought it was cold just with my shins in the water—a spine-deep shudder racked my body at the freezing water.

No, I tried to remind my stuttering body—n-n-n-ot f-f-f-reezing. If it was freezing there would be ice. It's not frozen it just feels that way. It's not frozen. You can do this. You *have* to do this.

Get moving.

Get the *fuck* moving. NOW.

I crawled soundlessly the rest of the way into the lake. Then I scooped some mud from the bottom of the lake and shakily smeared it over my hair, hiding the blonde as well as any residual smell from my shampoo. And then before I could crawl whimpily out of the lake and start screaming at the top of my lungs, "I give up!", let some old, wrinkly bastard "blood" me, then fuck me with his limp-viagra-made-just-hard-enough-to-fuck-his-trophy-for-the-night-in-a-surely-traumatic-manner just so I could get warm again—

I started to swim.

I would think about the plan. Nothing else could enter my mind. Certainly not the cold seeping so deep into my bones I didn't know bones went that deep.

The plan. *Right.* I needed them following the old, stronger scent from when I was still wearing the cloak. I didn't know a ton about dogs trained for hunting and tracking by scent, but I figured they'd untangle the scents soon enough and be on top of me before I was ready.

The lake was large with several twists and inlets. I could feel the buttplug foxtail dragging in the water behind me, tugging against my anus. I squeezed tighter around it, not wanting to lose it in the water. The fact that I'd forgotten about its presence for even a moment was just more testament of the evening's insanity.

There was no moon tonight, and with my hair

and face covered in mud, I hoped I was effectively invisible against the dark water.

Where was Sully? I suddenly wondered. Was he out there among all the other mounted men, hoping for his chance at *first blood*?

No time to think about that. Focus. Onwards. One stroke, then another. Don't disturb the water too much. *You're just another ripple of the wind on a very, very cold, but not-quite freezing, January night.*

I stuck to the edge of the lake opposite from where the men were and swum the length of it, back towards the manor house.

Out of the blue, dogs started baying wildly in the distance. Voices raised excitedly.

No doubt they'd located the spot I'd spread the scent around. That meant I didn't have long before they discovered the cloak in the trees. They'd realize I'd tried to trick them and be twice as resolute to catch me, then doubly furious when they did.

My foot touched down against the lake bottom. I'd made it to the other side. But if I scrambled out, it would be obvious this was where I exited.

I bit my lip, and even though it cost me precious time, I backtracked a little bit to where a low-hanging branch swung out over the water. Even better, tied to the branch was a swinging rope with a couple of knots tied in it, dangling about a foot above the water.

A summer pastime, now my salvation.

Climbing an old, knotty rope while naked and sodden was not my idea of a good time. The drenched buttplug foxtail dragged me backwards down into the water. I had to clench it extra hard to keep it in place.

But last year Tanya had gotten on a health kick, and while we couldn't afford a gym membership, we were able to create an area on the back porch for what she called *Country Strong Cross-Fit* (LeAnn nicknamed it *Red Neck Cross-Fit*)

Tanya tied a rope very similar to this one now confronting me to the ceiling of the porch in addition to other stations—we'd lift concrete blocks, run up and down the country road with ropes attached to old blown out tires slowing us down, and would repurpose any bit or bob we could get our hands on and MacGyver it into workout equipment.

Tanya forced me out there with her every morning at six a.m.

I was useless at the rope climb the first three months. But finally, with enough reps of those damn concrete blocks, and pulling those tires, it finally happened—I was able to pull myself a third of the way up the rope.

A month later I could make it almost to the top. That was last December.

Tonight, in spite of my exhaustion and fear, adrenaline spiked right when I needed it to. I hauled myself up and out of that bitch-twat-cold water, hand over hand on the rope. One hand and then, grinding my teeth together and straining all my muscles, *pull*, and another hand up.

I ignored the burn of the rope against my delicate palms. We always taped up for this at home.

But just thinking about Tanya and Reba and LeAnn—they were my power and my strength. They always had been.

I pictured their faces and I hauled myself up that damn rope.

Hand over hand, and *pull.*

Reach, and *pull.* The wet fox tail slapped against the back of my thighs.

Reach, and *pull.*

Not scream-growling with the effort was half the battle. But nope, not one damn sound would eek out of my mouth to give away my position.

I couldn't hear the dogs anymore, and the voices had quieted down, too. I couldn't obsess about what that might mean.

I just kept reaching upwards into darkness.

Until finally, *finally,* my hand hit the bark of a tree branch.

Hauling my body up and onto the branch was a task more brutal than any yet. The whole time I was terrified someone would notice the swaying tree branch.

But at a certain point, all I could do was the best I could. This was my best chance, and I was at the limit of my capacity. It'd either work or it wouldn't.

I finally swung all of my body and hefted my leg up and over the branch. And then I was sitting on top of it rather than dangling from below. I could have laughed with relief. But all I gave myself was two Mississippis to rest, then I climbed higher to another branch that stretched out the other direction—over land instead of lake.

My arms were jelly when I finally climbed out and hung from it, dropping the last few feet back to the ground.

Don't you dare, I warned myself as my limbs almost gave out. *Don't you fucking dare.*

I hadn't just dragged myself across a near-freezing lake for nothing. It was only sheer force of will that kept me on my feet. Because goddammit, the less exposure of my body surface to anything else that could catch my scent, the better. It would probably be pretty obvious where I entered the lake, but I was hoping all this effort would keep them confused for a little while about where I exited.

The ground was newly mown here, and one protip Sully did tell me was that freshly cut grass was one of the few things that could confuse a dog on a scent trail. And because the Order was sporting like that—aka, they liked it when their Human Hunts took longer—they always made sure to get the grass cut the day of the hunt.

The manicured lawn was also kinder on my bare feet. But I had to be careful, because maybe one of those bastards had thought about all this and was lying in wait. *Bastards*. This game was as much of a mind-fuck as it was grueling physically.

I ran low and close to the ground as I headed back for the shining beacon on the hill of the lit-up manor house. The wet foxtail of the plug occasionally slapped wetly against my thigh, but I forced myself to ignore it.

Going for the ridge might have been the smarter move. But I'd never been the smartest girl, had I? And there was no going back now.

I was tired and exposed and did I mention *tired*? No, make that exhausted.

If I could actually manage this—trick them by doubling back so they wasted a few hours hunting in the woods, all the better. Because I simply couldn't keep this pace up. My arms were burning from the rope climb, and the adrenaline was starting to wane.

My legs, though, they still had a little bit of fight left in them.

So, I ran, bent over low, and until all was quiet again, noises of hounds and horses far in the distance. Then I sprinted for the cellar where the little note had indicated on the map. It even had a crude drawing on the back showing how to get in.

I ran around the East wing and snuck around the outer garden that was used to harvest vegetables for use in the kitchens. And there, finally, I found it. The entrance was all but hidden. It doubled as a storm shelter, but of course the Order couldn't have something as pedantic as a storm cellar marring their property grounds.

I rushed to the entrance by the garden and pushed with all my might against a statue of a naked Venus. Because God-forbid their vegetable gardens be anything other than Georgia Historical Tour worthy, naturally.

I needn't have pushed so hard. The statue slid easily and quietly to the side, obviously on some sort of track I couldn't see, revealing stone steps that led down into the darkness.

I clambered down them without even thinking twice.

I only reconsidered and wondered if I'd just

jumped from the frying pan into the fire when the dim light of the night that my eyes had long adjusted to cut off completely.

Because the statue slid into place behind me and then I was surrounded in darkness, complete darkness. And no one in the living world knew where I was.

I knew she was smart.

Thank God she was smart.

I had hoped she would go to the cellar, and when I watched her muddy frame sneak behind the statue and disappear into the darkness, I couldn't help but release the breath that I'd been holding.

Hearing the hounds in the distance, I acted quickly and followed her. Raising my gas lantern to see into the dark room, it only took a second to spot her wide eyes and wild stance.

When she recognized that it was me who had found her, she relaxed and didn't appear as if she would pounce with claws out and ready for a fight.

"So, you found me," she said, as she crossed her arms against her chest.

"Would you rather it be someone else?" I strode across the room and placed the light on an old wooden table. The warm glow lit up the room enough that I could see how dirty and exhausted Portia looked. Mud caked her hair, and her body dripped water and shivered before me.

I removed the ridiculous frock coat I was forced to wear for the hunt and placed it over Portia's shoulders.

She pulled it tightly around her, but her teeth still chattered. "How did you find me?"

I didn't feel the need to tell her that I had written the note and hidden it in her cloak pocket to find. I had been part of these hunts before as a boy and knew exactly what they did. I knew she needed the advice on how to beat these limp dicks at their own game. I had considered just outright telling her myself, but I doubted she would trust or listen to me. But a letter from a fellow belle... well, I had just hoped she'd be smart enough to take the instructions to heart.

I shrugged in answer, hoping she wouldn't push it more. It was important that she feel empowered as much as possible right now with all things considered, and I wanted her to feel as if she had the power alone to outrun and outsmart the hunters.

"So, what does this mean now?" she asked, moving on to another question.

"I've won the hunt," I said. "Free drinks for a year, it seems." I waited for one of her classic smart replies, but when I got nothing but a shivering and frightened girl, I realized it wasn't the time to jest. "Are you okay?"

"Why wouldn't I be?" she snapped. She lifted her arms and spun in a circle. "I mean... look at me. Don't I look perfectly all right?" She took hold of the tail and pulled it out of her ass with a grimace, tossing it to the corner of the room. "I'm sick of this place. I'm so over the Trials. This isn't worth it. I can't keep going and doing awful stuff like this hunt. For what?"

"I understand. I'm sick of it too," I said softly. "But we have to stay focused. It's easy to walk away. Trust me. I've considered it more times than I can count. But at the same time, it means those fucks won. It also means that everything we've gone through"—I motioned at her wet and dirty body—"everything *you* have gone through up to this point would be for nothing if we both leave here empty-handed. We deserve something for what we've already endured."

"Oh, so now I'm not the gold-digging whore anymore?" she asked on a huff.

"Not any more than the rest of the world."

Her eyes seemed sad, and her small frame appeared dwarfed in my jacket. This wasn't the spitfire I was used to standing before me. The hunt had clearly taken its toll.

"I'm losing myself," she said. "I don't even know who I am anymore. I have absolutely no control over anything and—" She sighed loudly. "I feel like I'm selling my soul to the devil... or devils in this case."

"You are." I nodded in agreement. "No way to sugarcoat that fact. We both are."

"Which is why I'm considering telling the Elders to go fuck themselves. I have sisters at home who need me." She stopped speaking and looked down at the floor. "I just don't know how much more of this sick, twisted madness I can tolerate."

"Try to remind yourself why you accepted the invitation in the first place. It helps me when I want to storm out the front doors and never look back." When I saw she didn't seem to be getting any warmer with my coat, I closed the distance between us and wrapped her in my arms to offer some body heat. "The cellar is too cold. Let's get you out of here."

"What about the hunt?" she asked as she nuzzled herself into me.

"I won. It's over."

"What about the others? The dogs? I can still hear them looking for me."

"Let them hunt. Frankly, let's keep the fuckers out all night searching for you. When they find us, I'll already have you in my possession. I'm sure they thought this would be easy. Well... let's make the shitheads work for it."

"I like that idea."

Picking her up and cradling her in my arms, I said, "I want to take you to a place I went as a boy with my friends. It'll take them a bit to find us there since I know we already covered the rocky ridge earlier hunting for you. It would require them doubling back which will really piss them off."

"I can walk," she said, but she didn't try to resist or wiggle out of my arms.

"They'll be looking for your tracks. Not mine. I'm going to ditch the horse too, just to be extra safe." I nodded at the lantern. "You can hold that and light our way."

"What about the tail?" She scowled in the direction of the corner it was tossed in.

"Leave it. You lost it during the hunt. Not your problem."

"The Elders won't get mad?"

"Nowhere in the rules does it say you have to keep the cloak or tail. They may not like the fact you don't have any of it still on, but they can't claim you did anything wrong or it being worthy of failing the Trial."

The sound of the hounds was getting louder, and I knew we had to act fast or risk the night ending. As much as I wanted a hot shower, our bed, and the Oleander walls protecting us from this barbaric ritual, I meant it when I said I wanted the members to have to suffer a bit. It had rained earlier. The ground was a muddy mess, and the mosquitoes were out for vengeance. Muggy hunting wasn't a fun activity, and no doubt they all were dreaming about a bourbon and a blowjob right about now.

I sure as fuck wouldn't mind a good ol' B and B. But since I had to carry a muddy girl to a hidden cave and had to be uncomfortable, they sure as fuck would be too.

"How did you find me?" she asked me again as we made our way to the ridge.

"You're smart. I figured you'd come to the cellar." I repositioned her weight so that I could make sure the jacket kept her covered as much as possible.

"Am I getting too heavy?" She wrapped her arms around my neck as if that would help.

"I'm in shape now because of you. All our morning exercise has helped with my so-called pudgy gut," I said with a smirk. "And no, you're not too heavy." I sped up my pace just to prove my statement, plus I wanted to reach the cave before our lantern light was spotted from afar.

"Do I stink?" she asked. "Because I really feel like I stink."

I laughed out loud and shook my head. "No, you don't stink."

"I may never get this mud out of my hair."

"If I remember correctly, there's some water that drips into the cave. It forms stalagmites or stalactites or whatever they're called. But there should be enough for you to be able to clean off once we get there."

We walked the rest of the way in silence, the only sound being the barks of far-off hounds. So far off, that I knew we would have a couple of hours of safety before the hunters began to retrace their steps. When the cave appeared, I couldn't help but smile at the memories that washed over me.

Montgomery, Beau, Rafe, Walker, Emmett, and I loved coming to our secret clubhouse. No one knew about this place—at least that we knew of— and we liked that it was all ours to explore and hang out in. Some of the parties we were brought to at the manor were so stuffy that we couldn't wait to run out and play in our special cave. The Oleander wasn't all bad. In fact, there was a time when all of us boys couldn't wait to be a member of The Order of the Silver Ghost. It was a rite of passage like losing our virginities. It wasn't something any of us dreaded but looked forward to.

I had admired my father so much. We all did. We all wanted to be them when we grew up. My father could do no wrong in my eyes although I rarely got to see him. Which was why I loved coming to the Oleander as a boy. At the manor, I would at least get to be in the same room with him, or at the very minimum, the same house. He worked all the time and was rarely home. So, to me, the Oleander was better than home. It meant I had my father near. And he enjoyed having me there. All the fathers liked their sons to be present at all the appropriate parties and rituals. We were their lineage. We were their legacy. And there wasn't one of us boys who didn't want it more than anything. I used to dream about the day of joining The Order of the Silver Ghost.

Of course, then we grew up and opened our eyes.

Either that, or something changed. It was hard to imagine generation after generation of highly-educated, Ivy League men would condone all of these sexist, animalistic, and perverse acts. It wasn't just money that seemed to take over the secret organization, especially since everyone who joined the Order had money. It was the need for *more* money. The need for power and frankly... world domination. Greed oozed from the Oleander rather than heritage. The Order of the Silver Ghost lost its way, and I wanted nothing to do with it. Absolutely nothing unless I had to.

But I had to.

My sister needed me to.

And right now, as I entered the cave with Portia in my arms, I knew that she needed me too. Montgomery was right when he said we were a team and had to be in this together in order to make it. I had been a pretty shitty team player up to this point, and I didn't blame Portia one second for wavering and considering calling it quits. She'd been in this completely alone, and my drunk ass only made things worse.

But fuck it. That was all about to change. I wouldn't let these men break me, and I sure as hell wouldn't allow them to break Portia.

My belle would remain unbreakable.

I was happy to see a small stream of water running from the ceiling of the cave to a small pool of water. My memory had served me correctly. The air was cool, but not terribly cold, and I was pretty sure anything was better than being on the hunt in Portia's eyes.

"You can't hear the dogs in here," Portia said as

I placed her on her feet. "We won't hear them coming."

"It doesn't matter. We have plenty of time." I pointed at the water. "Shower off. You stink." I gave her a wink, a slanted grin and then took the lantern out of her hand and placed it on a flat rock.

"Jerk," she teased back, but shed my jacket and did exactly that.

It was fair to say that Portia Collins had become my sex partner, fuck buddy, hook up, or whatever you wanted to call it—at least at the Oleander. We fucked because what else did we have to do besides that? Not to mention, I was a man. Call me what you will, but she was gorgeous and there was no way I could resist the urge to bury my cock inside of her every time I woke up to her sleeping in my arms. But watching her stand beneath the water rinsing the mud from her golden hair, I didn't want to fuck her.

I wanted to hold her.

I wanted to protect her.

I wanted to make promises that no man would ever touch her in any way... except me.

The surprising emotions washing over me were raw. Primal.

The overwhelming need to somehow mark her as mine and mine alone, seemed to suck all the air from within the cave.

Droplets of water glistened on her flesh under the warm light of the lantern, and for the first time this evening, Portia seemed content again. Her strength seemed to return as she allowed any weakness she once had to wash off of her with the mud.

"You mentioned you had sisters," I said, feeling like I had to say something to break the silence.

She looked my way as she squeezed her hair, pulling the last bits of mud from the tips. "I did?"

"In the cellar."

"Oh... well, yes. I have sisters." She went back to washing her hair, no longer looking at me. "What about you? Siblings?"

"I do," I said, wondering why she seemed to not want to talk about her family, although I didn't really blame her. I didn't feel like going all in and discussing Jasmine either. "I have one sister."

Silence again.

It dawned on me that Portia and I didn't really talk about much. Definitely nothing of importance. Up to this point, I enjoyed that fact, but for some reason I wanted to know more about her. Maybe it was because I brought her to a special place of mine. The cave had been off limits to girls. It was our bro code, although I was pretty sure my friends would forgive me. But I was sharing a piece of my childhood... or as close to sharing as I truly ever got.

"Do your sisters know you're doing this? The Initiation?" I asked.

"Does yours?" she countered.

"Yeah," I said as I found a rock to sit on. "You can't be brought up as a VanDoren and not know about the Oleander, The Order of the Silver Ghost, and all the other fucked-up crap that comes with it. It's part of our Southern charm, I guess you could say."

"Why do you want to be part of the Order if you hate it so much?" she asked as she stepped out of the water and grabbed my jacket off the nearby rock and put it on.

Good question. Why?

Insanity.

Rape of will.

Forced obligation.

"Fate. Destiny. I don't know. Bred into it."

"So, you *don't* want to be part of the Order?" she asked as she came and sat down near me.

"It's complicated," I said, always hating that statement, but it was the only one that really described me and my situation. "What about you? Why are you truly putting yourself through this? What's the dollar amount?" I tried hard not to sound judgmental, but instead hoped it came off as the genuine question it was.

"It's complicated too." She froze and her eyes widened. "Did you hear that? I think I heard something outside."

Standing up, I walked toward the entrance of the cave. I signaled for Portia to remain where she was. I didn't hear the hounds but that didn't mean a member of the Order hadn't broken away from the pack like I had in hopes of having better luck solo. The darkness made it tough to see much further than a few feet ahead of me. I considered calling out but wasn't sure I was ready to face the Order yet.

"I see tracks leading to this ridge," a voice called out. "Get the others and the dogs. She may be hiding in these rocks. Let's flush our little fox out."

Fuck.

We didn't have the time I thought we would. I turned back around and entered the cave. "Take off my jacket and hand it to me," I ordered as I walked toward her with my hand out. "They're coming."

Portia stepped back and tightened the coat around her neck. "What does that mean?"

"It means, I can't have you wearing my jacket." When she didn't instantly give me the coat again, I clarified, "I hunted you down, remember? You're *my* win. Don't give the Elders reason to believe I helped you in any way."

Her eyes were wide, and I could see her lip begin to tremble, but she removed the jacket and stretched her arm out for me to take it.

Clearing the last steps between us, I softly touched her upper arm, and then stroked her cheek as I looked her directly in the eyes. "You're going to be okay. Trust me on that. I won't let them touch you. You're mine. I found you."

Without giving her a chance to say another word, I bent down and flipped her over my shoulder, carrying her as one would carry their prey. Her bare ass rested next to my face, and I figured the display of me carrying my captured fox like a bag of potatoes would please the Elders.

"I found her!" I called out as I exited the cave. "I captured the fox!"

It wasn't long before we were circled by the members of the Order all on horseback. I had hoped to keep them up all night searching for her, but it had been hours since the hunt first began, and I could see the men were weary and pleased that the fox had finally been found.

"I see you know your belle's scent well," one of the Elders said with a wicked grin.

"I found her in the rocks," I said, pleased that I had headed the Order off before they found us in the cave. Maybe some knew of our special place, but it gave me satisfaction that I at least shielded the secrecy from the hunting party.

"The little vixen shed herself of the cloak and the tail, I see," another Elder commented.

I placed Portia onto the ground and decided to distract the group with my next action before they could start criticizing or discussing her lack of cloak and tail and if there should be ramifications for that act.

I looked Portia in the eyes and prayed she could read my thoughts. I needed her to trust me. I needed her to remain quiet and allow me to handle everything. I needed her to submit to what I was about to do.

Taking out my pocketknife from my pants, I grabbed her hand and faced her palm toward me. "I won the hunt," I declared.

I sliced the blade along her palm, holding it firmly when she hissed in pain and wanted to pull away. A crimson red streak coursed along her flesh, and I hated that I was the reason for this wound. Swiping my fingers into the cut, I then smeared my bloody fingers all over my face, marking myself with the hunted's blood. I then took her hand again, swiping at the remaining blood from the wound, and wiped it down her face as well.

"She's mine," I proclaimed.

The members of the order cheered at my victory and my blooding. They were also no doubt celebrating that they could now partake in that bourbon and blow job they'd been fantasizing about since the evening's festivities began.

The fox hunt was finally over.

And the prey was definitely mine.

11

SULLY

A part of me wanted to go to the Billiards room with the rest of the Order for the bourbon and blowjob they were all going to partake in as was tradition after a fox hunt, but I also didn't feel that was fair to Portia. The poor girl had been through Hell, and I really didn't want to leave her alone after all of that. I also had an odd and primal need to protect her.

I didn't want her out of my sight again.

Not while we were still at the Oleander.

And no man, not even for a game, would hunt and terrify this woman again.

I would not ever let her feel the way she had as long as I could help it.

I would protect her.

The stakes were higher now. We were one step

closer to the end, and the reality was sinking in. There was no way we would make it until the final day unless we acted as one.

"I'm going to run you a bath," I said as we entered our room. She wasn't as dirty as when I first found her since she had rinsed off in the cave, but her body shook from the cold, and she needed warmth all the way to her bones. Her blood was all over her face, from my own doing, and it was at the very least my job to remove it.

She nodded as she wrapped her arms around her nude body. I was getting used to seeing her naked, but I hated seeing her vulnerable.

Naked was sexy as hell, but vulnerable pulled at my heart and made me want to make it right. I couldn't fix everything, but I could at least make her warm.

After checking a dozen times if the water was the perfect temperature, I added a couple capfuls of bubble bath to try to end her night in a little less horrific way. I then went to the sink and washed her blood off my face, trying to not focus on the macabre elements of the situation.

"I've never wanted a bath so much in my life as I do now," Portia said behind me as she entered the bathroom.

"You may want to test the water," I said,

standing up. "I've never run a bath for anyone before."

"I'm sure it's perfect. Thank you," she said as she walked over and put one foot into the tub slowly.

I walked over to the edge of the tub and held her arm to help steady her as she got in. I wasn't sure exactly why I was helping her into the bath as she was more than capable of doing it herself, but again... something about the fox hunt had changed me. I wanted to treat this girl like a fine piece of china.

As she lowered herself all the way into the water, the bubbles covering her nudity, I said, "I'll leave you alone."

"Wait," she called out. When I turned around to face her, she added, "Do you mind staying in here and talking to me? I don't really want to be left alone with my thoughts."

I leaned against the counter and nodded. "I can understand that. If your thoughts are anything like mine, then they're pretty haunting."

She ran the bubbles up and down her arm, not looking at me. "They are. Everything changed when I got here. I thought I could do this. I always considered myself a strong person, and there wasn't anything I couldn't do when I set my mind to it. But tonight really made me question that."

"Which is the intent of the Order," I said. "They want to break the belles. This is all a sick game to them."

I grabbed a washcloth from under the sink, walked over to the tub, dipped it into the bubbling water and began washing the blood from her face. I didn't want to overstep, so I handed her the rag so she could continue the job herself, but I found it odd that I didn't want to stop.

"You continually speak as if you aren't part of it. As if you aren't wanting to be them. I just find that hard to believe."

"I've never wanted to be them since I was old enough to see how fucked up they were. Never." I repositioned my weight from one leg to the other as I leaned against the counter again. "I know you think I'm just some entitled rich kid, and this is my dream to be part of the all-powerful Order of the Silver Ghost. But you couldn't be more wrong." I walked over to the edge of the tub with a cup I grabbed from the sink. "Let me wash your hair."

She didn't resist or say anything as I reached for the bottle of shampoo.

"I've never assumed to know you, Sully," she said, tilting her head back while I poured water over it and began massaging shampoo into her hair. "You're as much a mystery to me as the Order and the Oleander are."

"I like long walks on the beach, Labrador dogs, and a cognac by a raging fire," I played. The conversation was getting far too serious for my comfort. "And apparently I like washing the hair of pretty blondes."

She giggled. "Well, this blonde thanks you. I'm finally starting to feel normal again. If the intent of the Order was to make me feel beastly, then they succeeded. I actually felt like a feral animal out there on the run."

"Those assholes are sick in the head," I said as I rinsed out the shampoo and reached for the conditioner.

"Sully?" she said softly. "Do you think we're going to complete the 109 days?"

I released a deep breath. "I do. I don't think it's going to be easy, but I think you and I have something going for us."

"What's that?"

"We're both stubborn asses."

She laughed. "You're right about that."

"And we both don't want them to win. If we lose... Well, I don't want to hand them that satisfaction."

"Nor do I," she said.

"Well, then let's make a commitment that no matter what, we complete the Trial and refuse to allow them to break us."

"Deal. Us against them."

"Us against them," I echoed.

My next moves were guided by a man who genuinely had feelings for the woman sitting in a pool of bubbles, locked in a mansion of hate.

This wasn't me. I didn't nurture. I didn't care. But Portia deserved for me to do exactly that. She was owed gentle, she was due kindness, and she had earned devotion.

At least for now.

At least for tonight.

I helped her out of the bathtub and wrapped a fluffy towel around her. Her big eyes looked up at me in a silent thank you.

No more aggression.

No more harsh.

No more edge of a jagged blade.

Not tonight.

I brought her over to the counter and reached for her brush. Not asking permission, but not feeling I had to either, I ran the bristles through her hair. She watched my actions in the reflection of the mirror in silence.

We didn't speak.

But we didn't need to.

Right now, we just needed each other.

We were in the middle of a game not for every-one. It was a nightmare we endured together. We shared something that I'd never share with another. I needed her. She needed me.

If I was mean to her, then that meant I was being mean to myself.

We were one now.

At least in the Oleander.

As I combed through the final tangle, she turned and kissed me as gently as I had been combing her hair.

I wasn't planning on fucking her tonight. That wasn't my intent. Not after everything she went through tonight. But as she dropped the towel and stood damp and ready before me, she gave me no choice.

I needed to be inside of her.

She definitely gave me no other option when she began shedding me of my clothing.

"I need you," she whispered between our kisses.

We needed each other.

Once my clothes were off, I picked her up and sat her on the bathroom counter. She wrapped her legs around my waist and drove her tongue deeper into my mouth.

I ran my fingers through her hair and resisted the urge to tug. I liked rough sex, but not tonight. Tonight was about her. Making her feel safe and cared for.

Spreading her legs wide, I lowered myself down between her thighs. Inhaling deeply, drowning my senses with her essence, I kissed.

"Sully..." she purred as she took hold of my hair, and it was her turn to pull.

The muscles in her thighs constricted, encouraging me to continue on. My kisses turned to licks as I circled my tongue over every inch of her smooth pussy lips. She cried out and pressed into my face as my mouth found her clit.

As a reward for her visible and audible lust, I inserted two fingers into her pussy as I swirled my tongue with the goal to make her cum on my lips.

"Oh my god, Sully..." Her words came out as pants and her legs quivered around me.

"Come for me," I ordered as I pumped my fingers in deeper. I wanted to do nothing more than to simply give her pleasure.

The submissive side of her instantly complied with my command. Her mewls grew in intensity as she jerked her hips beneath me in a moan of completion.

Before she could fully get her breath back, she said, "I want you inside of me. Now."

I was never one to take direction from others, but in this case, I would most certainly make an exception. Not wasting another minute, I stood up and positioned her body at the edge of the counter so I could thrust my hard cock inside of her.

As much as I still wanted to be gentle, the animal inside of me escaped the cage.

Over and over, I fucked that tight pussy of hers not ever wanting to stop. The carnal need to merge my body with hers overpowered every other emotion. Her tight muscles constricted around me as she cried out another orgasm. Her body moved with mine, milking me toward my own release.

Never had I truly felt like I belonged in the arms of one particular woman until this moment. Yes, I fucked her with lust and passion, but there was so much more. We were at battle and stationed on the same side. We had a common enemy, a common goal, and a common prize at the end.

Montgomery said we would be a team. He knew exactly what this felt like, and I had chosen at the time to ignore, even fight against it.

But now.

This moment.

I didn't want to have another soldier beside me except for Portia Collins.

12

PORTIA

The walls were closing in, causing complete madness.

It was the only way to describe what was occurring between me and Sully. We went from hate to... well, something completely opposite, in a matter of days, hours, even minutes. It was like a yo-yo of emotions, and I didn't know how to process it. I could only imagine he might be feeling something similar. I most certainly couldn't read him, or even understand him no matter how hard I tried.

Today... he was weird. Distant, but not mean. We were awkward, but not cold.

I had been in the bathroom getting ready for tonight's Trial. Neither of us even had a clue as to what it would be since I had been given a sage green dress that reached mid-thigh. It wasn't slutty, and considering I was usually naked, I was considering it a win. Though who knew in this place. I knew better than to take anything for granted.

"Easy access," Sully had murmured, running the tips of his fingers underneath the hem and brushing my ass. I shivered, but otherwise chose to ignore the comment rather than snapping back with some witty comeback. I was figuring out I didn't need to always fight back when it came to him. I much preferred the white flag that waved between us as of late.

As I was applying my lipstick in the bathroom, I heard a knock on the door and then Mrs. Hawthorne's voice entered the room. I considered leaving the bathroom to greet her but chose to put my ear to the door and spy instead since I could hear she and Sully were already in conversation.

"You need to be nicer to that girl," she lectured. "She deserves more than being treated like an animal."

"With all due respect, Mrs. H—"

"That's the problem, laddie," she interrupted sharply. "You don't show anyone any respect at all. I get it. You're going through a lot with your father's death and all, and so I'm trying to give you and your poor attitude a long leash before I pull it back in. But don't think for a second I won't. Just because you're a grown man, doesn't mean I won't box your ears."

"My father has nothing to do with my *poor attitude*."

I could hear them both clearly, but even so, I wished I could see the standoff between them.

"Your father has everything to do with how you behave, and trying to ignore that fact isn't doing you any favors," she said.

I heard a deep sigh come from Sully; a sound I was getting quite used to. "Mrs. H... I really need to get ready for tonight."

"Yes, you do. Which is why I'm here. Tonight is going to test the both of you, and you need to be there for that girl. She needs you. You need her."

"I get it."

"I don't think you do, Sully. You put up this wall, but the Order is going to break it one way or the other. I just don't want you to destroy that poor girl in the process."

"I have no intention of hurting her. And for the record, I'm trying to be nicer."

"Well, try harder," Mrs. H said. "All I'm seeing is an ass. You're better than that. You always have been. Don't become your father."

"I'm nothing like my father," Sully barked.

"I beg to differ, sonny. You'll let the darkness from his soul enter yours if you aren't careful. You better learn to silence those vices of yours and how to soothe the hate in your veins."

There was a short period of silence, and I wondered if Mrs. Hawthorne had left the room, but then heard her speak again.

"Stop fighting everyone, Sully. We aren't all your enemies."

"You would fight if you were in my position as well."

"You aren't the first young man to be going through this. But you are the first one to have such a foul disposition about it."

"And you think what is happening is right?" he asked.

"It's not for me to judge. But I will say this... it's your ancestry. It's your lineage. It's your job to figure out how to adapt and overcome both. You can't run from who you are. You can't hide. I know you think running off to play surfer boy in California was a good way to do so. But you have responsibilities. You have a sister and a mother who need you now more than ever before."

My ears perked up. Sully had briefly mentioned having a sister but gave very little details about her. Was she older or younger than him? He was always so closed off with me about his personal life or anything before he showed up at the Oleander.

"It's time you step up and be a man. This Initiation in The Order of the Silver Ghost is about that. Being a man. It's time."

The door to the bedroom opened and then shut. Mrs. H had left.

I waited a few moments and then walked out of the bathroom not sure what kind of mood I would find Sully in. He struck me as the kind of man who didn't appreciate being lectured by anyone, but I was pleasantly surprised to find him standing in his tuxedo, a hand in his pocket and a smile on his face when he saw me.

"You look amazing," he said. "Really pretty."

I looked down at my short dress and silver heels and smirked. "At least I'm not wearing a collar, a fox tail, or some other kinky costume."

"*Yet*," he countered with a wink. "The night is young."

He extended the crook of his arm for me to take and led us out of the bedroom and to the ballroom. Even though I had done this walk many times, I still felt nervous. It was the unknowing. The surprise. I couldn't prepare.

Sully was the first to speak when we entered the room. "Fuck." His entire posture went stiff as a board.

I followed his gaze to a man sitting down next to a leather chair with a tattoo gun ready. The

Elders stood around the tattoo station with canes in hands as if they were prepared to beat us if we said no to what was to come. The chandelier lights were dim and a fire burned in the large fireplace on the right side of the room that had yet to be lit since being here. It was like a scene from some fucked up black and white gothic movie.

"Are they going to tattoo us?" I asked, mentally preparing myself for it.

Sully released a deep breath and led us to the chair.

"Gentlemen," he said to the Elders. "Is this where I get a pink butterfly tattooed on my ass?"

"Sully VanDoren," an Elder spoke. "You are first."

I expected Sully to put up a fight, but he surprised me when he sat down, pulled up his sleeve, and rested his wrist in front of the tattoo artist. It was clear he knew what was going to happen and had already accepted his fate. He knew what was coming, and even knew where the tattoo was to be given. Then again, the man did grow up in this twisted world.

I, however, still had no idea what was going to happen. I took a step closer to Sully so I could see as the artist began the tattoo with the buzzing of the gun echoing off the walls of the ballroom. The

Elders stood in place, eyes on Sully, as the tattoo of two crossed sabers marred his wrist.

Sully didn't even flinch. He sat so stoic I silently questioned if it would actually hurt when it was my turn. I was pretty sure there was no way it wouldn't hurt to have a needle jammed repeatedly into my wrist at a million points, but at least Sully didn't seem to be in agony.

He kept his eyes on me. I wasn't sure if it was so he wouldn't have to look at the Elders who I knew made him sick to his stomach, or if I somehow kept him calm, but I liked it. If I was his focus point, then I would dutifully stand next to him and appear strong for his sake—even though I was internally shaking.

Here I was about to get my first tattoo in front of a bunch of old dudes in cloaks, and there wasn't anything I could do about it.

I think I would have preferred a pink butterfly on my ass to what Sully was being given, but I was pretty sure I could somehow cover the tattoo with bracelets until I could get it removed or altered to be something less nightmarish.

When the crossed sabers tattoo on his inner wrist was finished, and the gun turned off, the sound of canes hitting the floor rattled my bones.

I was next.

I took a deep breath, locked eyes with Sully and nodded.

I could do this.

"Portia Collins," the Elder spoke. "It is now your turn to get the Mark of the Order."

Sully impatiently waited for the artist to wrap his tattoo, and then he stood up and took my hand. He leaned in and whispered in my ear, "You don't have to do this if you don't want to. I would understand if you said no and wanted to turn back."

I pulled away so I could stare directly into his eyes. I needed him to see how serious and determined I was. "A tattoo is not going to stop me."

I sat down in the chair Sully had just been in and sought comfort in the heat of the seat left from him. I was ready to get this over with, but the tattoo artist stood up and gathered his equipment to leave.

In confusion, I looked at the Elders. Wasn't I getting a tattoo, too? They'd just said it was my turn for me to get my mark, that I was next.

But then, one of the Elders walked over to the fireplace and pulled out the long handle of a metal poker that I hadn't even noticed nestled in the hottest embers of the fire. On the tip of the metal was a brand of two crossed sabers.

"Absolutely fucking not!" Sully shouted, clearly seeing what I saw but comprehending it quicker than I did. "You aren't burning her. No fucking way."

I choked as soon as I got it. They actually wanted to— They were going to— To—

But I couldn't even finish the thought before Sully was storming the Elder and knocking the poker out of his hand in rage.

"Sully VanDoren," an Elder from behind me called out. "You will contain your anger or lose this Trial and the Initiation will be over, causing both you and Miss Collins to leave the Oleander as losers."

Hearing the threat was enough for me to shoot out of the chair and rush to Sully before he ruined everything for the both of us. No, he couldn't! I couldn't let him!

"Sully," I reached for both of his hands. "Sully," I all but shouted when he seemed to not even notice I was standing in front of him. His eyes were focused on the Elders like he was plotting each of their deaths... in detail. Gory detail. Crap. I had to get through to him. "We aren't going to let them win. Remember?"

His furious eyes refocused on me. "You are not going to sit there and get branded like some sort of cattle. I won't allow it." He glanced at the Elders and then back at me. His glazed eyes focused on my face. "Tell me how much money you want. I'll write you a check right now so we can get out of this place and never look back."

Oh, Sully. I shook my head. "What about you? What about what you're here for?"

"Fuck it all. There are some things not worth it. And this is too much. It's fucking sick!"

I squeezed his hands in hope I could somehow lend some of my sanity to his out-of-control rage. "They can't break me."

That I knew. Not when so much was at stake. I'd never let them. "And they can't break you." At least I prayed not.

But no, looking at his fury, his iron rage and will—I knew they'd never break him. Who could stand against Sullivan VanDoren and win?

He yanked his hands out of mine. "I just said I would pay you whatever it is you want. I have the fucking money!"

"It's not about the money," I countered, hoping that the Elders were not going to deem this Trial a failure because we were taking too long to act.

"Sully," I lowered my voice, hoping he would hear my urgency. "We need to do this."

"Are you fucking kidding me?" he shouted. I wasn't sure if he was saying the words to me, to the Elders, or to all of us. Probably all of us. Or maybe he was shouting it at God. "Branding, Portia! They're trying to fucking *brand* you!"

I needed to act quickly. There was no way I was going to be able to convince Sully that we should do this, and the more we stood there, the more at risk we were of the Elders pounding their stupid canes and announcing the Trial was over.

So, I did what was necessary. Just like I always did.

I was *not* my fucking father.

I stayed. I did the difficult thing. I made the difficult choices because I knew what love was.

I walked over to the cooling red-tipped poker on the ground and picked it up. I handed it to the Elder who had first held it.

"Go ahead and do it," I said, extending my wrist. "Get it over with." My voice only trembled the slightest bit.

Sully marched to me and took my arm, pulling me toward him with more aggression than I had ever seen before. "I said no!"

I all but bared my teeth at him. "Well, good thing I wasn't asking for permission."

"So, you have no limits to get your payday? Is that what you're telling me?" Sully's jaw clenched, palms fisted, and his body tightened so much it appeared his spine might snap.

"I'm telling you I refuse to be broken!" I yelled.

His rage had finally rubbed off on me, and if I

didn't focus my attention on the branding, I would completely lose my shit on him.

The Elder had already reapplied the poker to the fire and had pulled it out and handed it to Sully who only stared at it. The tip glowed a golden, burning yellow-orange again. Smoke burned my eyes from it and the air shimmered near the heat of the tip.

"Sully..." the Elder began. "It is your responsibility to brand the belle in order to complete the Trial."

Sully darted his eyes to me, to the hot branding iron, and then back at me. "Is this what you want? Really want?"

"Do it," I snapped, as I extended my wrist.

"On the hip," the Elder said, pointing to my hip bone.

I took a moment to process the new location on my body that would permanently be scarred, but actually preferred it over my wrist. So, with that, I lifted up my short dress, and glared at Sully, willing him not to chicken out.

"They won't win, Sully. Don't let them," I said in a low voice.

"So fucking sick." He glared at all the Elders in the room. "You guys are sick bastards. How do you sleep at night?"

He then took the brand from the Elder and brought it close to my hip.

He considered doing it. I saw that.

And then I saw the revulsion shudder his entire body and what a violation of his soul it would be to press it against my skin, to harm me like that.

Sully could only be pushed so far. He was a bull of a man. And they'd just reached his breaking point. He'd burn down this entire manor before he ever applied that brand to my skin.

So, I reached forward, wrapped my hands around the poker high enough where I prayed it wouldn't burn, and yanked the brand flush against my own fucking hip.

Burning metal, burning flesh.

Barbeque.

It smelled like barbeque. *I* smelled like burning meat.

I howled in agony and threw the brand away from my flesh at the same time Sully yanked it back in complete horror.

Pain, blinding, hip on fire, fire burning up my right side. Fire, I was on fire. FUCK IT HURT; I WAS ON FUCKING FIRE—

My leg muscles gave out.

Arms from behind grabbed me before I fell. *Their* arms. *They* were holding me. Not Sully.

Sully was still standing in front of me, horror

on his face. Why wasn't he holding me? Sully. *Sully. Get their hands off me!*

But I couldn't quit or refuse. Goddammit, I'd come this far, I'd overcome this Trial. Nothing and no one would beat me. No one.

The last thing I remember was silence, darkness, and a fire burning so deep on my hip that I wondered if the pain would ever end.

Fire, fire, I was burning up in fire…

I wasn't sure how long I wallowed in the shadows of this misery, but when I finally opened my eyes, Sully towered over me. I was in our bed, and he sat on the edge of it with worry painted over every inch of his face.

"She's awake," he called over his shoulder in a mixture of relief and fear.

Mrs. Hawthorne walked up behind him and placed her hand on his shoulder. "Oh good. Looks like she's getting some color back in that pretty face of hers too."

"Are you okay?" Sully asked, running his hand over my forehead and through my hair.

"What happened?" I asked, not sure how I ended up in our room and in our bed.

"You fainted, lass. Completely expected considering what you went through," Mrs. Hawthorne answered.

"How are you feeling now?" Sully asked, reaching for my wrist and checking my pulse. He looked up at Mrs. Hawthorne. "I still think we should call a doctor."

I shook my head and tried to sit up, only to have Sully push me back down onto the pillow. "No doctor. I'm fine." I glanced down at my body and saw a bandage on my hip. The burning sensation was still present but not nearly as bad. "I'm okay." I was a little breathless as I said it, but really, the pain was so much better than it had been earlier, it was shocking.

"There's burn ointment on that wound of yours," Mrs. Hawthorne said. "It will fix you up in no time. Heals like a charm."

"I should have never allowed them to do this to you," Sully said, scowling at me.

"You didn't allow anything," I said, forcing myself up to a sitting position. "I make my own choices, and this was one of them."

"That's right, lass. You keep that fight in you, and you'll walk out of here with all your dreams. Don't let those men gain the upper hand." She gave me a smile, patted Sully on the back, and said, "If either of you need me, I'll be in the kitchen."

I didn't watch her leave because my focus was

on Sully who still sat right beside me. His brow was furrowed, dark circles underlined his eyes, and he appeared years older than he had been just yesterday. I leaned in and kissed his cheek. We'd survived. Thank God we'd gotten through and to the other side.

"Don't worry. I'm fine," I repeated. "*We* are going to be fine. But we need to stay strong. There is nothing we can't get through. Nothing."

"Never again," he growled. "Do you hear me? I will never, ever hear you cry out in pain like that again. I will kill before I'd ever let that happen. Never. Ever. Again."

He pressed his lips to mine and gave the softest kiss.

I kissed him back so I wouldn't have to agree to his terms. I had no idea what was still to come, and if I had to scream and sob and beg on my knees and endure pain after pain before this Initiation was over, I would do it. I would do it all.

Because nothing could be worse than what would greet me on the other side if I failed.

13

Mrs. Hawthorne had lectured me to be nice. I knew I needed to be nice.

But fuck that.

I was fucking pissed. Raging. Furious.

And as much as I wanted to hold Portia, kiss her softly, whisper promises to her that I had no power to keep, what my darkest soul wanted to do was scream. I tried to hold it back. The poor girl had been burned after all. Her delicate flesh seared and singed. She needed comfort. She needed softness.

But fuck that. My fury was too big. It was a monster inside me.

"What are you thinking?" she asked, taunting the bear. She didn't want to know what I was really thinking.

"Why didn't you take me up on my offer?" I asked, trying to control the anger that nearly blanketed every single syllable of my question.

"Offer?"

"I offered you the money you wanted so you wouldn't have to get the brand."

She darted her eyes away from mine and then took a deep breath. "And I told you there was more to this than money. If you'd just be a little more patient, I could—"

But the boiling fury inside of me finally bubbled over. "Patient? You fucking branded yourself! You did it to yourself! Are you so much a whore you can't even see the madness of what you did?"

Her mouth dropped open in shock, and then the same fire from the end of that fucking branding iron entered her eyes. Finally, fucking finally.

"Back to calling me a whore huh?" she snapped, eyes afire. "Call me what you want, but if it weren't for me, we both would have failed the Initiation tonight. Your weak ass couldn't handle it!"

Weak? I was the only one standing up to those twisted bastards.

"Who gives a fuck?" I shouted, jumping up from the bed and pacing the room like a caged tiger. "Who fucking cares? There are some things in life that—"

"No!" she shouted from the bed. "Quitting is not an option. Do you hear me? We. Can't. Quit."

I ran my fingers through my hair and concentrated on breathing. I needed a fucking drink. I need a hate fuck. I needed to run from this place and never return. I needed escape from my reality, from my past, and from my fucking future.

But only one of those options was possible.

I was going to fuck the greedy whore locked in this room with me.

Not asking. Not waiting. Not hesitating in the slightest, I charged the bed and began tearing her clothes off in a wild fury.

She could have screamed. She could have said no. She could have tried to fight.

Not that any of that would have helped.

But instead, she met my rage, my aggression, my fury head on.

"I'm going to fuck you until you cry out," I growled, getting her naked with every word.

"Good," she said.

"I'm going to make it hurt."

"Good," she growled furiously back at me.

"I'm going to treat you like the whore you are."

"As long as that means you won't act like the coward you are," she countered.

Fucking bitch.

Seeing red, I flipped her onto her stomach and licked my palm as it would be the only lube she'd be getting. "You better finger yourself, play with your clit, do whatever you need to get that pussy wet. I'm going to fuck this ass of yours until you scream for mercy."

"Make it hurt," she mumbled against the pillows on the bed.

I swiped my licked palm along her pussy and collected the juices that were already there to lubricate her anus with her own arousal. My whore liked it rough, it seemed.

And just as I took hold of my shaft and placed it at her puckered hole, I froze.

I wasn't this man.

I wasn't my father. *He* would fuck a woman in the ass with no care in the world. *He* would call a woman a whore. *He* would be an aggressive asshole with no control.

I was not my father.

I was not my fucking father!

Hopping off the bed, I struggled to untangle myself in all the partially discarded clothing, hating myself for what I'd just been about to do.

"Wait," Portia cried out. She sounded confused, half-pissed, half-vulnerable. "Don't go."

"I have to," I said, pulling up my pants. "I don't

trust myself around you right now. I can't control the rage I have. I feel so fucking out of control." If I didn't leave, I was going to punch my fist through a goddamn wall.

She reached out for my hand. "Take that rage out on me. I want you to. I want you to fuck my ass. I want you to get every piece of anger out of you. I want this." She tugged me to the bed. I dared lift my eyes to meet hers, and I felt it straight through to my fucking spine when she said, "I need this just as much as you."

I didn't have the strength to say no. And she was right. We both needed it. We needed some way to release the tension that threatened to strangle us both. And fuck knew I wanted inside her—inside that tight ass of hers more than anything I'd ever wanted before on this side of the grave. I kicked off my pants but did walk over to the bedside table first and pulled out a bottle of lube. The girl had just been branded and she didn't deserve a dry ass fucking no matter how angry I was with her.

I didn't want to think. I didn't want to woo. I didn't want to comfort. I just wanted to be buried balls deep inside of her ass, and judging from how Portia lay on her stomach, with her tight ass on full display... waiting... she wanted it the same way.

I coated my dick with lube as I said, "I'm not going to be gentle or slow."

"Good," she said as she looked over her shoulder at me with a sinful grin. "I'd rather have that sting than the sting on my hip."

Mounting behind her, I guided my cock to her asshole—fuck me what a beautiful little perfect asshole—I wanted to thrust my thumbs in and feel all around. To stretch her and intrude into her secret places but I was too impatient, and my steel-hard cock needed inside more.

Needed to fuck. Needed to be fucking her now.

My cock started pushing inside her hot flesh. Even though I said I wouldn't be slow, I did ease up when she gasped and gripped the bedding in her fists. The crown of my cock was not small, but her tight anus was. So tiny. She had to groan and relax and allow me to really work it to wedge it inside her body.

We had to work together, and at some point there was nothing for it but for me to jut my hips forward and *breach* her.

She cried out like a mewling kitten when I did, and a groan from so deep inside me rumbled out of my throat. Fuck *me*, nothing felt as good as being in her sweet ass. Only her pussy could compare, but they were each perfect in a different way. Now that I'd had her ass, I'd never let it go. I'd be demanding to come back here all the time, or as often as she'd let me. Maybe it'd only be on special occasions and fuuuuuuuuuuuuuuuck—

I thrust in deeper and then pulled out again.

Her entire body spasmed and her fists clenched the blankets so tight her knuckles turned white. More ecstatic noises came from her throat.

"Keep going," she cried out. "Cum in my ass."

God this woman...

I inched my way deeper and deeper, feeling her inner walls clench around me. I wasn't going to last long, but with how tight she was and how much I was stretching her, I was pretty sure she didn't want a marathon ass fucking anyway. I was happy to see her reach around and begin to stroke her clit as I pulled out only to push back inside again.

Her little cries came out higher and higher pitched and she writhed beneath me. Our bodies slid together, and I bent my forehead against her arching spine.

I latched onto her shoulder blade with my mouth, then my teeth as I shoved in deep again, a long slide of my cock against the silky inner walls of her ass, her clenching around me, clenching and releasing, clenching and releasing as she stroked her pussy and her clit.

I tried for a steady pace but couldn't manage it. There was never any steady with her, no matter how hard I tried to find my absolute control.

Instead, something else happened. She soothed the ever-before restless beast inside me.

With every staggered stroke, my anger dissipated. With every thrust, my fury fizzled. With every moan and sexy mewl escaping from Portia's lips as she brought herself to climax while I ravished her ass, I saw this woman for what she was.

Not a bitch.

Not a whore.

A goddamn survivor. A treasure.

She was strong and powerful.

She was a woman bringing me to my knees.

And if it weren't for her... we wouldn't still be in the fight.

I bottomed out inside her, a hard thrust that made her cry out in both pain and pleasure, and spent my cum deep, deep inside her most secret place.

14

I couldn't handle another branding. Although at this point, who knew? Who the fuck knew what I could and couldn't handle?

When I'd first walked through those doors, I would have said I could take anything, no matter what. For my family, I would endure anything. Any pain, any emotional torture, *anything*. For family, one could endure it, because that's what love was. Real love.

And now?

Now... well, I was counting the cost. My flesh was burned, and I remembered the sound of it sizzling and the feel of the arms holding me while I screamed. It was a mark I'd carry with me forever.

Was it worth it?

Absolutely.

Would I do it again?

...

Probably.

But I was also glad there were no time machines. I was glad it wasn't a choice I'd ever have to choose again.

Except for the fact that we'd just been graced with another Invitation.

We were cordially invited to another night of sin and debauchery downstairs and the question ringing through my head was—how much of my blood would it require this time?

The Fox Chase really could have been so much worse. I'd gotten out of it with just a few scrapes. The branding would scar me for life.

What did tonight's little soiree have in store for me?

Sully had been withdrawn ever since we'd gotten the invitation, last night's amazing primal sex notwithstanding.

But right before we headed downstairs, he reached out and grabbed my hand. I was surprised and I must have looked it.

"I won't let them hurt you again," he said. The determination in his brow said he was very serious.

I melted inside. And I wanted to tell him no, not to make that sort of promise, it was one he couldn't keep, one I wouldn't *let* him keep, but then he was pulling me out the door and down the stairs.

The dress code on the invitation had just said "Elegant Evening Attire + Carnivale Masque"—so Sully was dressed in a black suit with the top few buttons of his pressed white shirt unbuttoned. It was sexy, but then I suspected I'd find the man sexy even if he was dressed in a sackcloth and ash.

I was wearing a tight red dress that hugged my curves with enough cleavage on display that Sully hadn't been able to take his eyes away after I'd put it on but not so much that I'd be embarrassed if I wore it to church. Not that I ever would, cause red on a woman was the devil's color, I'd been informed many a time by my sexless Sunday School teacher as a small child.

As we came down the stairs, I realized "Elegant Evening Attire" was being loosely interpreted by everyone in attendance. Oh, sure, most men were in suits and tuxes, but the ladies on display, well, they were a whole other story.

Sure, they were all elegant, to a one. And everyone had a mask on. Some sparkling with jewels, others, simple black silk masks. Most had some sort of elaboration. Feathers. Ribbons sewn in. One had a large honking nose extended as if it were a plague mask. A couple of men wore masks that were grotesque in other ways, satanic almost.

The women wore masks that were almost all just strictly beautiful. White. Red. Peacock colors and features. Probably from a real peacock, knowing this crowd.

But as far as the rest of the women's attire... Well, elegant diamonds dripped off of one dark brunette who was sitting as the centerpiece in the center of a round table. A sparkling necklace dripped diamonds down between her exposed breasts, almost all the way to her belly button. Her legs were open wide and the only other thing she had on was a string of pearls around her waist, looped with another strand that dipped down between the lips of her pussy.

Masked men took turns playing with the pearls, tonguing them against her clit and lapping at her cunt. Sometimes another player would pour champagne down her body and multiple men would lap at it, like dogs all fighting for the tastiest morsel.

Everyone in the room seemed to be in another world. Not like people usually looked when they were drunk, but not exactly sober. Their bodies were so loose, their eyes so bright.

"Absinthe, sir?" A beautiful waitress with an elaborate golden carnivale mask paused in front of Sully. She held out a tray of little cups filled a third of the way with bright green liquid, along with a few other objects.

Sully started to say no thank you but the woman leaned in, whispering in Sully's ear. I wanted to punch the chick for her audacity—he was obviously here with me—but then I heard what she was saying. "It's expected. Montgomery said to tell you they're expecting you to drink."

"Fuck," Sully swore. Then he nodded tightly. "Fine." He reached for one of the little glasses but the serving lady pulled it back.

"You aren't wearing your mask."

"Jesus Christ," Sully swore, then pulled two crumpled masquerade masks out of his back pocket and handed one to me. His was black with a golden detailing. Mine was white with the same. They were both far less elaborate than the others in the room, but I was frankly glad for it. I would hate to have to focus on keeping one of those giant masks with the feathers on one side balanced all night.

I put on the simple, elegant white mask as the woman with the absinthe led us over to a small side table.

She expertly arranged two little absinthe cups, and then, laying a cute little spoon over the top of the glass, she suspended a cube of sugar in the center. Then she poured something on the sugar so that it partially dissolved and stirred the sugar into the absinthe.

"What's that?"

She smiled wide and did not answer as she handed Sully and me the two glasses she had prepared. All she said was, "May you have a glorious evening reveling in the expansive pleasures of the body and the mind."

Sully rolled his eyes. "Yeah whatever."

Then he looked at me, clinked tiny glasses with me, and smirked.

"Bottom's up!"

I glanced at everyone in the room again, and then at Sully. "Is this drink why everyone seems so... I don't know... off?"

When I looked at the little glass a bit skeptically, he just laughed. "Come on, just take it like a shot. Get the burn done with. Like ripping off a band-aid. If we're not going to fight them, we might as well join them and enjoy the ride."

Okay, well it wasn't like I had a choice. I nodded at him, and then together we both threw back the absinthe like a shot.

The green liquid *burned* down my throat. I immediately started coughing and gasping for breath.

Sully started laughing his ass off at my reaction.

Which made me want to punch him, so I did—just on the shoulder but still!

"What was in that?" I barely squeaked out, my throat still on fire.

He shrugged. "Knowing these men... anything. I'd guess poison except they all seem to have drunk it."

"Water," I wheezed through my burning throat.

He finally stopped laughing and took my arm. The serving chick was nowhere to be found, naturally. Sully led me through the maze of mostly naked party revelers, and finally found a big pitcher of cucumber water. He poured me a glass and I downed it, then put the cool glass against my suddenly heated cheeks.

We stood in silence for several minutes, hours... I had no idea. My mind spun and my body soon hummed in a bizarre way I had never experienced before.

"Good God," I whispered, covering another cough with my wrist, "who would drink that on *purpose*?"

Which made Sully start chuckling all over again. "I used to think your cuteness had to be an act, but I'm starting to think it's just genuine. You can't fucking help it."

I glared at him. "I. Am. Not. Fucking. *Cute*."

His lazy grin just got bigger. "Are too."

"Am *not*." Why did I feel like huffing and stomping my foot right now would do nothing to prove my case? Oooooooh, I *really* wanted to slap that grin off his face.

Or fuck it off him. Fucking it off of him would also be an *excellent* option.

I bit my lip and felt my cheeks heat. Time to look away from the very fuckable man. Yes. Do not continue that train of thought. No sir-ee.

"Well, what the fuck was that?"

I looked over at Sully in surprise. "What?"

"Whatever thought just made you blush like a virgin?"

My mouth dropped open and I looked away from him, no doubt my face blooming even pinker.

"None of your business!" I whispered. But then suddenly Sully's hot hand was at the back of my neck, massaging just underneath my ear. And then he was leaning in and whispering at the back of my other ear, his breath tingly and hot.

"What was in that drink?" I asked. Even my vision seemed to be affected all of a sudden. Everything was so bright, and my body surged with life. "I shouldn't feel this way from just one drink." The rational part of me was fighting this overwhelming need to be... giddy.

"Does it matter?" he asked with a smile as he blinked several times, clearly feeling the way I was.

"We drank it. We might as well make the best of it."

"We should get back to the party."

"You mean the party where everyone's fucking each other? Where they're touching and cumming on each other, but those dumb fucks don't have even an ounce of the chemistry that's blazing between you and me?" His tongue crept out and licked the bottom of my earlobe. "You mean *that* party?"

My breath hitched, my entire body spasmed, and I think I came right then and there.

I spun in Sully's arms and my hands fisted in the lapels of his suit. Suddenly I felt drunk on him. God, his *lips*. They were so full and rough, and I knew juuuuuuuuuuuuuust the way he liked to use them on my body.

I bit my bottom lip hard.

Because it wasn't just his lips he liked to use.

Oh no, Sully was a fan of using his teeth. All over my body. Nipping and biting. He was such a naughty boy. Didn't he know good girls didn't like to be bit?

But then maybe I wasn't such a good girl after all? Because I *did* like to be bit. Maybe I was the kind of girl who liked wearing red to church on Sundays. Maybe I was the kind of girl who wanted men to look at her—no, I just wanted *THIS* man to look at me.

I wanted him to look at me the way he was looking at me now—like he was about three seconds from ripping every stitch of clothing I was wearing off and fucking me so deep and so hard I'd never feel anyone else on my body because it would never feel right because no one else would be HIM.

I lifted my gaze from his lips to his eyes…

And was slammed by the wall of echoing lust and want and fucking desperate NEED.

He grabbed me up by the waist and my legs locked around his hips.

He dragged me from the room like a goddamned caveman.

We crashed through the door into the study. Another couple was making out against the wall but Sully roared, "GET OUT," in the most authoritative, sexy voice I'd ever heard and they went scurrying.

But he didn't throw me around. He was careful as he laid me down on a plush rug in front of a fireplace.

I didn't want gentle, though.

I wanted the animal in him to mate with the animal in me.

I ripped at my fancy fucking red dress that probably cost so much in regular times I'd be appalled by the waste. Not tonight. Not now. I grabbed it at the dip of the V in the cleavage and ripped downwards. When it barely tore, Sully helped it the rest of the way, rending it all the way down the middle.

We were both just as impatient with my underwear and so anxious with my bra we just shoved it down so he could drop his head and latch on to my nipple while he impaled me with his cock.

The second he thrust inside me, we both gasped in relief.

Not that it was enough. It wasn't nearly fucking enough.

"More," I moaned. "Harder." I ripped off my mask and then his too. I didn't want anything between us. Nothing covering even a millimeter of those amazing eyes of his. I needed it all.

He was already nodding, bracing one hand on the floor above my head and curving the other around my ass so he could notch himself even deeper inside.

"Yeah, baby, I'm getting there," he murmured. "I know what you need. I'm getting us there, baby. I got you. You know I always got you."

I nodded and buried my head in his chest, but that wasn't nearly enough. I lifted up so I could meet his mouth with mine.

For a moment he gave in, tangling tongues hard as he thrust in deep, claiming me in those animal fucking thrusts just like I needed. He always knew just what I needed. Fuck yes, right there, just like that—

"Yes, honey, oh yeah, right there, ooh, right *there*—" My voice went hypersonic as I came again, legs clenched around him, the heel of my foot digging into his ass and pulling him in tighter.

He redoubled his pace, fucking me into the soft carpet and the hard floor beneath so good, so goddamned good—

I clenched and came again, and that was his fucking breaking point.

He pumped into me and swore, "Fuck, best I ever had, fucking golden pussy, never want anyone else, never, best, perfect, you're perfect, fuck I adore you, fuck, oh fuck, only you, always you, only *you*, here it comes, oh fuck, oh fuck oh fuck oh fuuuuuuuuuuuuuuuck!" The last word was a shout, and he clutched my body to him. I clenched around him as we hit that sweet hot fucking light together and exploded into a million fucking pieces.

Sully slumped over me, breathing so heavy.

I was busy floating.

Right up out of my body, somewhere up around the ceiling.

At the same time, I was in my fingertips. In them!

Tingling. Floating. Swirling.

There were colors. So many colors.

My soul was giggling.

This drink... what was in this drink to make me so... bright? Bright. Bright. So bright.

Sully so warm. Skin on my skin.

"I like you. So much," I confessed, my voice sounding foreign to my ears that felt... odd.

Sully shifted, a beautiful smile lighting up his face. He didn't smile enough. He should smile more. I reached out a finger and traced the beautiful line of his lips. Up one side of his mouth and then down the tip of his luscious lip over to the other side. Pretty pretty lip.

One of his heavy, sexy sexy eyebrows lifted. Did he hear me? Did I speak out loud?

"Pretty lip?" he asked. He sounded amused by me. But even as I watched him, his plum-chocolate eyes deepened and shone. He blinked and the smile dropped off his face.

"Why do I feel so... I feel different," I said, not hating it at all, but confused by how traces of light seemed to follow every one of Sully's movements.

"High. We're high," he said. Or did I just think he said it? "You're beautifully high. I've had absinthe before, and it was nothing like this. This is something..." He closed his eyes and stretched his neck like a lion straightening and expanding into its skin.

Then he opened his eyes, and they settled back on me like I was just the prey he was looking for. But it was more than that. There was a light, and a warmth, and a possession there. "This is something else," he whispered in his deep, rumbling bass that I loved. I loved how it rumbled from the chasm of his chest and vibrated into mine because our bodies were touching.

It was like he was seeing me for the first time all over again. But his usual masks weren't up. He looked... he looked in awe at what he was seeing.

I quickly looked over my shoulder, but no one else was there. It was still just me in the room.

He reached out one of his thick, sturdy fingers and ran it down the slope of my nose. I giggled at the feel of the touch.

And finally, his smile returned. "I like that sound," he murmured, his syllables seeming to drag out. Then he was climbing back over me.

I settled on my back on the carpet and he braced himself, sliding one of his knees between my thighs, elbows on either side of my head.

He explored my face with his fingers.

But his face wasn't like normal. He wasn't

wearing a sarcastic expression, or a smirk, or any other of his normal guarded looks.

There was this look of pure... concentration. He bit the corner of his bottom lip as he explored the line of my nose and then my cheeks, fanning out his fingers to explore my every contour.

And every point of contact felt like the sparkle-explosion of fireworks.

My nipples hardened to rock-tipped points.

Sully was between my legs and even though we'd just finished having sex, he thickened again, hard as stone against my inner thigh.

He made no move to do anything about it, though. He just kept exploring my face with the gentlest touch, in spite of his big, brutal fingers.

I came, my entire body arching up against him. I couldn't help it and didn't want to.

That got another smile out of him, one of the wicked, knowing ones I liked best.

And then his eyes moved down to my lips.

He looked completely mesmerized.

"Do you have any idea how absolutely fucking gorgeous you are?" he whispered. "You aren't anything like the other girls. You aren't fake. You aren't a Barbie. You're real. Jesus, you're so fucking real. You drive me crazy. You're all I can think about. I'm obsessed with you. I want to worship this body all day long."

He clenched my waist and down to my hips, massaging my flesh, but not on the side of the still-healing brand. On the other side, though, he massaged *deep.* "I want to make you feel so fucking good—"

He dropped his head and kissed me on the lips. Unlike earlier, it wasn't animalistic. This time, he barely brushed his lips against mine.

I moan-whined and lifted up for more contact. I didn't have to worry.

He kept brushing those thick, masculine lips of his against mine, closer and deeper every time. Tantalizing me. Driving me fucking beyond the brink.

Until I wrapped my arms around his neck and dragged him down to lock my lips with his. And wrapped my legs up around his waist just for good measure. We were still naked and slick from our first encounter. He slipped easily back inside.

I gasped and came with his first thrust and he licked and kissed down my throat as I clutched him through my waves of pleasure. My legs clenched around his waist, then notched up higher, knees high around his back, my heels against his ass. Grasping him to me with every part of my body I could reach. Closer. Deeper. Dear God, anything to get him deeper inside me.

"That's right, baby," he whispered. "Fuck

you're so hot. I'm taking you so high. You feel me? Feel how deep I am. How I'm marking you so deep as mine. No other man ever gonna have this pussy cause it's mine. That's right, you feel it. You feel me. You love me there. You know I'm the only one who ever belongs here. Who's ever gonna make you feel this. Who can ever give you this." He thrust in deep and bottomed out, exploring the depths of my inner contours with his perfect cock.

"Yes," was all I could cry. "Yes. Sully. Yes. Please. Oh God, please."

He latched onto my throat and sucked.

I squealed and creamed around his cock, coming again. I'd never been so responsive. I hadn't known I could come this many times at once. It was starting to turn into one blur except that wasn't even true. Each peak was spectacular. Taking me higher. Better than I'd ever had before, better than I knew was possible.

How was he doing this?

How were *we* doing this? We'd been having sex. I mean, we'd been having *a lot* of sex. And it was great sex.

But it was nothing like this.

I grabbed Sully's hair, rough, and dragged his face away from my throat. I had to see his face—his eyes, I had to look into his eyes and see if this was all in my head or if he was really here with me for this.

But fuck me—he was.

He *was*.

He looked at me like I hung the moon and stars. Like I was the Creator herself.

He saw me all the way down.

And I saw him back.

Neither of us looked away.

He continued pumping into me, as connected as two humans can be, and neither of us looked away.

I watched the strain on his face. He was trying to hold back the tide.

I cupped his face. Didn't he know he didn't have to hold anything back with me? He could have the pleasure today and again tomorrow and always forevermore.

We just found this and were never going to fucking lose it. I wouldn't let us.

This was unusual magic in this painful, tragic fucking world.

Everyone would try to steal it, stomp it, say it wasn't true, wasn't real.

We couldn't let them.

We had to fight for it.

I cupped his face in mine.

Oh, beautiful love, my heart sang, *fight for this*

with me. Don't leave me alone in this. We can have it all. I don't know how, but I know it's true. I know it deep down.

I communicated all with my eyes and I swear, for a second I swear he heard me. I saw the recognition in his eyes. He heard me and I hoped he'd be courageous enough to listen to my call to action.

I prayed he'd be courageous enough to fight for us. To fight for this once in a lifetime magic.

"Honey," he whispered. And then he closed his eyes and came so hard his entire frame shook.

I held him through the storm, one last orgasm washing through me.

Tears sprang to my eyes as I held my man, wept in pleasure, and prayed for a future I so hoped we could have, in a moment where everything seemed possible.

15

Those motherfuckers drugged us.

I knew there was more going on than just the absinthe, but there was really no choice in not drinking it. And as the night progressed, I knew it was far more intoxicating than normal. I had drunk my fair share of the green liquor in my lifetime, and never once had it fucked with my head like it did last night.

There had to have been some sort of hallucinogenic... LSD.

Likely. Thing was, once Portia and I got in that fucking study, I just stopped caring that I might not be in complete control of my own faculties.

It had taken most of the night for me to be able to actually fall asleep once we came back to our room, and even when I did, my dreams were so bizarre and vivid in color that I wasn't even sure if I truly rested.

And Portia. Poor Portia. Even sober, the girl couldn't relax enough to fall asleep quickly, so having her mind spin like mine kept her up even worse than me. I had held her, tried to soothe her, applied kisses when she stirred, but I knew she had just as much a restless sleep as me.

And what the fuck happened last night at the Trial?

We had the most amazing sex. Mind-blowing. Sex that seemed to last forever. Sex that took us to a level of... to a level of *what*?

My mind blurred with the memories, and as I glanced over at Portia in bed beside me who stirred awake, I instantly felt embarrassed. Last night wasn't just incredible fucking, at least not for me, and I seriously doubted it was for her.

Did I make a fool of myself?

What did I say?

What did I *do*?

Jesus Christ... Memories came back hazily. I'd called her *honey* and *baby*. I was... sappy as fuck. But the scariest thing about last night was I meant every single word I said. I felt it from the deepest shadows of my walled-up heart.

Was it the laced absinthe?

Or was it something more?

"Oh my god... That was quite the cocktail," she mumbled as she flung her legs off the bed and rubbed the drugged sleep out of her eyes.

"I think it was more than just a strong drink." I yawned and stretched but refused to sit up. "I think they dropped some sort of drug on the sugar cube."

Her eyes widened as she looked over at me. "Last night was... we were on drugs?"

"Maybe acid? Only way to describe what happened."

Her eyes diverted, and she cringed as if I had just reached out and slapped her. It took her a moment to lift her chin, push back her shoulders, and apply the fakest smile I had ever seen on her. "Right. Only way," she agreed.

"The Elders must have wanted to truly mess with our heads." I seemed to be upsetting her with my words, and I considered telling her I meant what I said last night—on drugs or not—and that I had felt—

"Nothing surprises me anymore." She shrugged and ran her fingers through her hair. "Everything about this place is lies, head games, and... laced with evil," she said as she got out of bed, walked straight to the bathroom, and closed the door behind her.

I released a sigh of relief. I didn't like that she stormed to the bathroom upset, but I also needed a moment to myself to process. I rubbed my jaw that ached from clenching my teeth so much last night as a side effect from some stupid drug, and I considered trying to fall back asleep in hope I could wake up again in a much better frame of mind.

When I heard the shower run, I knew, however, I didn't have long to languish in bed. Acid trip hangover or not, Portia was a morning person and would be expecting me to be up all bright eyed and bushy tailed.

Were we not going to discuss last night at all?

No soft embraces the morning after?

No sweet words?

Portia clearly didn't want to, and frankly... neither did I.

Last night was... well... it was last night and would stay that way.

Safer. Easier.

When the shower turned off, I groaned. The woman couldn't even take her time for that. Everything had to be now, fast, and on her own clock of efficiency. Knowing it was very likely she would come out in her workout gear ready to go, I decided to put a stop to the ridiculous idea of going for a run right after drinking poison. Grabbing the phone by the bed, I called the kitchen hoping I could convince Mrs. H to have some mercy and bring us breakfast to the room.

"I was wondering if I would be hearing from you, laddie," Mrs. H said on the other line.

"Yeah, last night was... interesting. Do you mind if we can have breakfast delivered? I would really owe you one."

"Of course. The usual morning after meal?" she asked with a good-natured chuckle.

"You know me so well."

I hung up the phone just as Portia exited the bathroom wearing exactly what I had expected. It amazed me she could just bounce back to her perky, avoidant self as if nothing occurred last night.

"I ordered us breakfast," I said, laying my head back down on the pillow. "It should be here soon."

"What about our morning run?"

"Portia," I groaned. "We're due for a day off. Especially considering what we took last night."

"Let's run it off," she said, opening up a drawer that held my workout clothes. "Sweat the toxins out of us."

"No," I moaned. I rolled over onto my side and pulled the blanket up over my shoulder. "I want greasy food and something to chase the hangover away. Hair of the dog is calling me."

"Sully," she whined. "Come on."

"Portia," I whined back, mimicking her tone.

"I want to run."

How true her statement was. She always wanted to run.

"Maybe you should try not running for at least *one* day," I said.

She slammed the drawer shut and threw my sweats onto the bed. "Yeah? Well, maybe you should stop trying to 'chase away' things for *one* day."

Touché.

Clearly, we were who we were and nothing— not even an intimate night—could change that. Especially when neither one of us were going to discuss what we said... and what we felt.

When she saw that I had no intention of getting out of bed, she huffed over to a chair and sat in it with her hands crossed. "Fine. After breakfast we go outside at least. I need fresh air."

"Fine," I said, wanting to give her at least something. She reminded me of a caged animal, and I didn't blame her one bit for needing to escape the suffocating walls of the Oleander.

We remained in awkward silence until Mrs. H arrived with our bacon, eggs, and orange juice that would soon be a screwdriver once I was done adding the small bottle of vodka that sat beside the glass.

Mrs. H looked at me, then at Portia and said, "Well, you sure do look a lot better than Sully does."

"Thanks," I murmured, but couldn't deny the fact that Portia truly lit up the room even in leggings and a tank top. "Love you too."

Mrs. H smirked as she placed the tray on the table by the fireplace. "You kids enjoy and let me know if there is anything else you need."

"We might need some more orange juice," I said as I sat up fully for the first time, trying to ignore the ringing in my ears.

"We have plenty of orange juice," Portia corrected. "We won't be needing anything else. Thank you."

I shot daggers at her and decided to not make an issue in front of Mrs. H, especially since it was likely Mrs. H would take Portia's side. "Thank you, Mrs. H. It all looks and smells great."

When the woman left the room, I got out of bed and considered walking over to breakfast buck naked just to really make Portia uncomfortable, but decided to put on the sweats she had tossed at me instead.

I was too tired, hungry, and still slightly drugged to be a full dick.

Portia beat me to the tray of food and took hold of the tiny bottle of vodka. "If I don't get to run, you don't get to chase away." She took a few steps away from me as if scared I would fight her for the booze. "Seems fair," she added.

I took a seat and reached for my plate, giving up on my morning cocktail. "Seems fair," I agreed.

16

I was feeling a little better after our last Trial as Sully and I walked down the stairs towards what faced us tonight. We'd had a few days off after the LSD.

Maybe this was the easy part of the Initiation, where they decided to take a break on us. They couldn't always be sadistic bastards. The whole point of this entire thing was pleasure, right? Absinthe, LSD, old men getting off in lots of new and interesting ways?

True, there was no Costume Box along with the invitation this time, so I would be naked. What else was new? The old men liked eye candy. Shocker.

I was young and scrappy.

They couldn't fucking brand me twice.

And Sully would protect me.

I glanced over at him and frowned. Things since the LSD hadn't been great between us. I mean, they hadn't been especially bad. But not great either. He'd been sleeping a lot. But not inviting me to bed with him. I did a lot of sit-ups and lunges and some of the in-room dance aerobics I remembered from YouTube videos Tanya and I used to do.

In short—we hadn't had sex since the LSD. After the morning after, I'd been so deflated when he told me the entire night... along with all the things he'd confessed to me, had *all been* because of the drugs. He'd said it so flippantly, like there was no possibility he could have said those caring, intimate things for any other reason.

I'd had to immediately flee to the bathroom so he wouldn't see the tears in my eyes. Because I'd thought—I'd thought—well, I'd been a stupid girl, hoping for stupid, stupid things.

I'd washed my face in cold water, gave myself a scolding in the mirror, but that wasn't nearly enough. There were still tears leaking uncontrollably out of my eyes, so I'd turned on the shower and took the hottest one I could stand, careful to keep my still stinging brand out of the water as much as I could. Eventually I'd given up and switched to cold water. Cold water in January was punishing but also felt entirely appropriate.

I'd only come back out when I had myself firmly under control.

And Sully had just kept acting like nothing had happened between us at all the night before. Maybe he hadn't even remembered saying those things. They were all still there in vivid, neon color in my head, but maybe the drug acted differently on everyone.

He'd been effectively ignoring me ever since. Even though I couldn't help contorting my body and flashing my ass in my tight shorts in his face a *bunch* during all those sweaty aerobics I was doing.

He just turned the other direction in bed, yanked a pillow over his head, and told me to put in some damn earbuds so he wouldn't have to listen to Britney Spears and Lady Gaga on blast five hours a day.

Then he thought when I climbed into bed with him at night he could just reach for me?

Uh... that would be a big *no*, buddy.

He'd just slept the entire day away, completely ignored me, then thought he could get with me because I happened to be a warm body in bed beside his lazy ass?

Nope.

Just because I was in this place didn't mean I'd

never heard of a little thing called self-respect, thank you *very* much.

But now that we were walking down the stairs towards the unknown, me completely in the buff and him stark naked too, I wanted to reach out and grab his hand.

They'd brought a suit for him like always.

He'd stared me in the eye and tossed it on the ground, stepped on it, and yanked off all his underclothes till he was as naked as me, then nodded towards the door when it was time for us to go.

And I'd fallen a little in love with the bastard.

When we both came into view of the Elders naked as the day we were born, I didn't miss the raised eyebrows. One man outright glared.

Not that Sully gave a fuck.

He just stood there in the full-naked glory that the good Lord gave him and smirked at all of them.

I started to get a nervous buzz in my tummy, and not the good kind.

There was some sort of... something in the air of the room.

Anticipation.

There was anticipation in the air.

Because while yes, some of the men were looking away from me, more of them were looking my direction. And grinning.

They were not grinning in a nice way.

Now I really wanted to reach out and grab Sully's hand.

But what would that accomplish? It would be a sign of weakness in front of vultures.

And he couldn't protect me.

Hadn't the branding shown me that?

I was here for a reason. Oh God, I was here for a reason. My family needed me. My family needed me.

I repeated it over and over in my head like a mantra as my entire body started to tremble in fear. I wasn't sure I believed in God, but I prayed for him to protect me anyway. Do what Sully cannot, I prayed. Please protect me. Save me from these evil men.

Just then, two women appeared at the door. They were naked, too. With beautiful make-up, perfectly shiny, blown out hair.

Southern belle sirens.

"Take her and prepare her," one of the men said. An Elder, I was sure.

The women nodded like little puppets and approached me. *No.* My entire body stiffened as alarm bells rang in my head.

"Where are you taking her?" Sully asked, a slight note of alarm in his voice, too. He'd seen my body go rigid.

"It's none of your concern," said one Elder

haughtily as another answered, "To prepare her for the Trial."

Sully looked toward a man in the corner. "Montgomery?"

The only other young one. Sully's friend. I looked toward him too, like he might be my salvation. He didn't look happy, but he nodded. "It's just a ceremony. It's fine."

Sully's eyebrows furrowed, but he nodded too.

I dropped my eyes to the floor.

His friend was a liar.

Or ignorant.

I hoped for Sully's sake that Montgomery was just ignorant.

And I also hated the man for not protecting me.

Because whatever they had planned for me was not going to be *fine,* I knew it deep down in my guts. I was not safe.

But I'd survived their Fox Hunt.

I'd survived their brand.

For my family, I would survive anything.

I turned away from Sully. I had a bad habit of not being able to hide my truth from him, and if he saw the truth of what I was facing, whatever evil it was, I feared he would tear down this manor.

But I had a family to think of... particularly my little sister. My dear, dear sister who needed me more now than ever before.

And her *life* was worth everything.

So, I walked to the sirens, the painted witches with angels faces, and I let them lead me through the door to what would no doubt be a new level of hell.

"No!" I screeched. I fought them. I fought them and I screamed.

Four men held me down at the end as they shoved me into the pine box in the ground at the edge of the property.

I screamed for mercy from the men holding me.

I screamed for help from the women who'd driven me there like a lamb to the slaughter in the golf cart.

I screamed for Sully.

I screamed for my long dead mama and the daddy who'd driven away from us when we needed him the most.

I screamed for God.

And not a goddamned one of them answered

me as they nailed the lid of that coffin shut on top of me.

I screamed for help until my voice was raw. I hated small spaces. I hated the dark, I always had. Oh Mama, I hated the dark. I *hated* the dark.

"Stop panicking, stop it!" I scream-whispered at myself with the tiny raspy voice I had left. "Fucking think!"

The box was pine. I was strong. I'd spent the last weeks working out. I was a strong bitch.

And I was a fighter.

God, my whole life was a fight. A knock-down, brutal fucking brawl.

Christina Aguilera's *Fighter* started playing through my head.

I was strong, and hard, and smart.

I started pounding at the box. It was just pine. Maybe I could bust my way out of the damn thing. I'd seen it done in movies.

I'd just save my fucking self. Like always. Save myself, and then save my sisters. I was one strong bitch, and if God wouldn't save me, I'd save my fucking *self*.

I was strong, I was tough, life was cruel, life was a goddamned *bitch*, to me, to my family, to my beautiful sister, and fuck it, fuck it ALL, I'd never give up, I'd never fucking give up—

I pounded on the wood above me.

I kicked.

I kicked more.

I pounded with my palms.

I tried to turn to get my elbows but I couldn't—

Dammit, I couldn't turn, the space was too small, there wasn't enough room, I couldn't— If I could just get some goddamned room, I was sure I could get the fuck out of here, but there wasn't enough space, I couldn't move my elbow, I couldn't get it, I couldn't get it—

Okay, okay, so I'd use my palms. Fine. Okay, okay—

I slammed my palms, but the wood didn't budge. It wasn't budging, I wasn't really doing anything.

But maybe with enough repeated hits, I'd weaken it.

I tried to kick again but it was the same problem, there just wasn't enough fucking space to get the right momentum to do any damage.

I screamed in fury, a useless noise with my ruined vocal chords.

And pounded more against the wood, uselessly.

And that's when the dark space suddenly flooded with light.

Light.

And I saw the scratch marks and at least one

woman's fingernail left embedded in the wood, inches above my face.

I wasn't the first woman they'd buried alive.

Oh Jesus, oh Jesus, they were fucking crazy.

There weren't any lines they wouldn't cross.

They hated us.

They wanted to torture us.

They liked it.

How many women had they buried?

Tears squeezed out of my eyes as I lost my shit and screamed and pounded and scratched in the same place how many other women had scratched?

And that was when the dirt started spilling between the boards.

I had no voice left beyond a useless, terrified squeak as they began to *actually* bury me alive, dirt filling my mouth as I screamed and spit and lost my ever-loving shit.

B illiards, bourbon, and blowjobs.

That's what I remembered about the room we were all walking to after they took Portia away. The billiards room was for members only, but as boys, we often snuck in the secret passageways hidden in the walls of the Oleander and spied on the men.

Oh, how I couldn't wait to be given the keys to that kingdom back then.

We used to fantasize what it would be like to someday be a member of The Order of the Silver Ghost. It was a given that we would have our opportunity when we came of age, but the day couldn't come soon enough as we watched these powerful men sit with their cigars, their wealth, and their absolute power.

I had desperately wanted to be one of them...

But not anymore.

The Order of the Silver Ghost was tainted. Poison. Absolute filth.

And as I walked buck naked down the hallway, I was proud of the fact that I would never allow myself to become one of them.

Never.

Yes, maybe I had to do the evil dance of the monkey for my sister's sake, but my soul would never be compromised by these men. Never.

"Sully!" Mrs. H called from the end of the hallway carrying a bundle of clothes and my shoes that were given for me to wear to the event. "Put that pecker of yours away and get dressed immediately."

Her face was bright red with embarrassment and maybe even shame as she rushed toward me and shoved the clothes into my arms. I tried not to smirk at her discomfort, but it was hard not to. Especially when I glanced over at Montgomery who was clearly holding back full-on laughter. My buddy found the humor in this situation just as much as I did.

I opened my mouth to ask where Portia's clothes were, and if she was expected to be naked, then so would I. Mrs. H put her hand up to stop me.

"Not another word out of you, young man!" Her tone was sharp enough to cut, and I obediently shut my trap. "Your mother would have a stroke if she knew I allowed you to stand here in the Oleander stark naked. Get dressed. This instant."

The rest of the members entered the billiards room—some chuckling, some scowling—as I put on my pants. I wasn't going to fight this spitfire of a woman, and I had already given the members of the Order the shock I had intended, so there was no need to go to war with the woman in the hallway who wouldn't hesitate to box my ears regardless of what age I was.

"Better listen to the woman," Montgomery said as he joined the others in the room.

"I swear, Sully. Sometimes..." she said as she spun on her heels and left me to finish getting dressed.

I couldn't wipe the smile off my face as I joined the Order.

One point: Sully VanDoren.

As I poured myself a glass of bourbon and took a burgundy velvet chair near the roaring fire, I said, "Well, gentlemen, what madness do you have in store for me tonight?"

I hated to admit it, but I did feel more comfortable now that I was fully dressed in my tux. I felt like I had a little bit more power as I crossed my ankle on my knee, casually leaned back in the chair and sipped the liquor as I waited to see what was next.

A blowjob maybe? Although oddly the thought of having some Order hooker sucking me off made my stomach sink. It seemed like I would be... cheating? Portia and I were not an official monogamous item... far from it. And yet, I couldn't explain why I only wanted her lips to be the ones wrapped around my dick.

"Yes, why don't we move on with the rest of the festivities for the night," one of the Elders said as he took a seat next to me. "Let's gather around and enjoy our evening movie."

He pointed to the empty wall on the west side of the room at which a projector was pointed. All the members who had been milling around either took a seat or positioned themselves in a place they would be able to view the projected film that had just been turned on.

The sound of Portia's screams filled the room before the image of her came into view. It took me several moments to make out what I was seeing before me.

It was Portia. There was a video camera wherever she was.

Screaming and scratching at wood above her. She was trapped somewhere.

"Let me out!" she howled as dirt fell upon her face. "Help me. Someone! Sully! Sully!"

The sound of her pounding against her wooden cage had me jumping out of my seat, my eyes locked on the image of her in misery and absolute terror.

"What the fuck is this? Where is she?" I boomed.

I stopped staring at the projection on the wall to look at the members of the Order for some sort of explanation but could still hear the cries of Portia echoing off every inch of the billiards room. Her distress reverberated off my bones as the horror of what was occurring sank in.

"Where is she? What are you doing to her?" I demanded as I lunged toward the closest Elder. I took hold of his collar and shouted, "Where the fuck is she?"

The Elder simply shrugged as he smiled at me in a taunting fashion. He knew I wasn't going to hurt him, and even if I tried, he knew the other members would step in before I could do any real damage to the man. I considered punching him just to wipe that smug look off his face, but Portia's continuing screams for help had me looking to another Elder for answers.

"I can't breathe," she cried. "I can't breathe!"

"Tell me where she is," I shouted. "Or I swear to God I will burn down this house right now!"

An Elder stepped forward and said very calmly, "Sully VanDoren, as powerful members in our society, we are often called upon to help others. It will be expected because of who we are and the resources we have."

He took another step as he pointed to the screaming woman clawing at the wood above her. "It is your job to save the belle. How you choose to do so is up to you. You can choose rage and try to demand answers you won't receive. Or you can choose a much more..." He paused and smiled. "Or you can actually help the belle."

I quickly glanced at Montgomery who simply stared at me with wide eyes. He didn't seem to know any more than I did, and if he did, he'd pay for not telling me. But I didn't have time to deal with this game.

I needed to find Portia!

I ran out of the room and sprinted outside. My gut told me where she was, and when I looked off in the distance where the old Oleander Cemetery was on the top of a hill by a weeping willow, I saw torches lit up.

Sick motherfuckers put her in the cemetery to join all the ancestors of the Order.

I had never run so fast in my life as I did that

moment. I couldn't hear her screams. Which meant only one thing.

They'd buried her alive.

The burning torches lit the way, and the disturbed earth told me exactly where I needed to dig. Of course the bastards didn't leave me a shovel or anything, so I had no choice but to fall to my knees and start frantically digging with my hands.

"Hold on, Portia," I screamed, not sure if she would be able to hear me.

I would have kept screaming to her, but I knew I was on camera as well and the entire Order watched on as I tried to save my belle. I wouldn't give them a show, and if I'd known where the damn camera was, I would have crushed it to pieces.

I dug and dug, struggling to breathe as if I too were buried beneath the ground right beside Portia. I made progress but not fast enough. There was another living being beneath me, and the thought of what she must be experiencing right now was a level of fear I couldn't even process.

I clawed at the ground with so much force that my fingertips bled, my nails lifted off the nailbeds, but nothing would stop how fast and furious I removed the pounds of dirt piled on top of her. They would have had to kill me to actually stop me. But just as I was beginning to panic my hands wouldn't be enough, and I considered running to the house to find a shovel, my fingers made contact with wood.

"Portia," I called out just as I heard her muffled screams. She was alive. Thank fucking god for that. "Hold on. Hold on!"

She was alive. I kept reminding myself of it. But at the same time, the Order had no intention of killing her. They just wanted to break her.

And after this...

She sure as fuck would be broken.

I paused for a split second before lifting the lid, worried that too much dirt would fall on her, but I couldn't think of any other way. I needed to get her out of this hole.

"Sully! Sully!" I could hear her scream as she continued to pound on the lid.

"If you can cover your face, do," I yelled against the wooden coffin. "I'm opening it."

Without waiting for a response, I removed the cover and pulled her shivering, naked body from hell.

In one swift motion, I lifted her out of the grave and held her so tightly against me that I could be the next one found guilty of suffocating her.

She sobbed against my shoulder, and I could do nothing more than stroke her back and kiss her dirty head.

"I'm sorry, so sorry. So sorry..." I kept repeating over and over. Every single minute she'd remained in that grave made me feel like a failure. I'd been so slow pulling on these stupid fucking clothes. If only I'd just yanked them on, they would have turned on the video quicker and I would have known. I could have gotten to her sooner.

She clung to me and once the sobs ceased, she pulled away and looked at me with wide eyes against dirt-covered skin. "Never be sorry. You saved me. You came and dug me out. I knew you would. I knew."

When her body trembled beneath my hands that refused to ever let her go again, I quickly removed my jacket and wrapped it around her. Just as I did, I heard a sound that nearly caused me to become homicidal.

The thumping of canes as the entire Order made their way up the hill like snakes slithering in the dark. Over and over canes pounded against earth as they began to chant something in Latin. Haunting voices, beady black eyes that were illuminated by the flicker of the flaming torches, and the stench of absolute insane madness.

The enemy had made its claim on my soul, and I refused to let them take it from me without a fight. With fury in my blood, I let go of a trembling Portia and charged through the darkened haze of evil and punched the first man who I felt deserved it the most.

Montgomery Kingston tumbled to the ground holding his face where my fist had just punched. I hoped the motherfucker's jaw broke with my force.

"You son of a bitch," I roared. "I expect this from these assholes, but from you? You?"

"You know what these Trials are like," Montgomery said as he stood back up, rubbing the sting from his face. "And for the record, I had no fucking clue what was going to happen. I would never do that to you, brother."

"You think that fucking matters? You think you can still call yourself my *brother*? You've become one of them," I spat. "I thought you were better than that. Just because you now wear a robe doesn't mean you have to be as fucked up as these old limp dicks."

"You're trying to become one of them too," Montgomery countered. His eyes narrowed and his jaw hardened. "Check yourself, Sully. You don't want me as an enemy."

Redirecting my anger, I stopped glaring at Montgomery and narrowed my gaze to the Elders.

"Are you happy?" I shouted as I took a few steps back and extended my arms wide. "Is this the outcome you wanted?" I pointed at Portia where she stood clutching my jacket around her, dirt-stained and shaking. "Is she scared enough for you? Did she scream for mercy enough while you all drank your bourbon and smoked your cigars?" I extended my scraped and raw hands. "Do you want me to spread my blood on her naked body?"

I marched over to where Portia stood, her mouth open and her eyes glassy with unshed tears. I parted my jacket, placed my palms on her breasts and ran them down her body, smearing my blood in a path of the blackest and darkest sickness.

"Like this, you sick fucks? Like this?" I spun on my heels and eyed each one of them in unleashed fury. "You all can go to hell."

Montgomery stepped up to me, which really took a set of balls considering I still wanted to strangle the man. "Settle down, Sully." He took another step toward me, looked at Portia and asked, "Are you all right?"

Portia came to my side and held on to my arm. I wasn't sure if it was due to her needing support or if she was trying to leash the beast inside of me that raged to be unshackled. I wanted to kill every single man who stood before me in their robes and with their canes.

"I am now," Portia said lightly.

Montgomery nodded and said, "I had to go through my own near-death Trial. I remember just how awful it was. They hung Grace at the gallows. I remember all too well. But you have to stay calm. Think bigger picture here, man. Don't let them push you to the breaking point. Don't allow it. Remember why you're here."

"Sully VanDoren," one of the Elders called out. "You have completed the evening's Trial. You are one step closer to joining The Order of the Silver Ghost."

"Fuck you all," I spat as Portia's trembling legs finally gave out on her. I caught her right before she hit dirt, hiking her up into my arms and marching us out of that damn cemetery. "I will never be you. Never."

I would fight until my bones gave out to not lose myself to this insanity. Yes, there was a bigger picture. My sister. I knew that. But I would never lose myself.

Had the Order broken me?

Yes.

Shattered the man I thought I was.

All that was left at the moment was a monster with the thirst for revenge. If I didn't leave with Portia, someone would get seriously hurt.

Something had to change. The Oleander had turned into a den of vipers, and I refused to be another serpent in its grips.

19

Sully's arms felt amazing around me. After the cold and the dirt and the death of that tomb they'd stuck me in, his life-giving arms carrying me to safety...

I curled into him. I tucked my face against his solid chest and listened to his heartbeat. He was alive and because of him, so was I.

I wanted to wrap my arms around him and never let go. Never, *ever* let go.

For as long as we both shall live.

We got to our room and Sully kicked open the door.

I hoped he would take me straight to the shower and cleanse me lovingly. I needed to be taken care of. I needed my strong protector to keep taking the lead. After that experience tonight, I seriously had nothing left.

But instead, Sully went into the room, shoved the door closed with his foot after us, and deposited me on the bed.

Okay, well, I was dirty, but I could understand his need to immediately connect with me after all we'd just been through. I could get with this new program. And I would welcome his body into mine with open arms. In fact, I was getting wet just thinking about it—

"What the *fuck* are you still doing here?" Sully all but shouted at me.

Whoa whoa whoa, WHAT?

I just blinked at him in confusion.

"How could you let them do that to you?" Sully went on. "What the *fuck* is so worth it to you that you'd let them treat you like an animal to bury in the back yard?"

My mouth dropped open. Was he seriously giving me this bullshit right now? Right *now*? After I'd just been buried the fuck alive? He was going to scream at me and accuse me, like it was my fault those bastards had shoved me screaming into that fucking box and started dumping dirt onto my head and scared the living shit out of me and—

I just started a slow clap. "Way to blame the

victim, Sullivan VanDoren. I'm so glad that *you* are such a bigger person, cause it's not like *you're* still here, too. Ever wanna take a look in the mirror, pal? You're trying to be one of the bastards who likes to bury innocent women in coffins. Who's the hero now?"

His face turned red. "You fucking *know* I want nothing to do with any of this shit!"

"And you think I do?" I screamed back at him. Except it barely came out as a whisper, because my vocal chords were still shredded from screaming for my goddamned life in that goddamned coffin and *fuck him* for giving me *any* of this bullshit right now.

I got off the bed and turned my back to him. "I'm taking a fucking shower," I said.

Then all of the sudden, he grabbed my arm and swung me around to face him. "Just tell me why."

His eyes were burning into mine, fury still written on his features. "Why are you here? What is it they have on you that could make you fucking stay for this? Cause I'm racking my brain and I can't think of a fucking thing that would make anyone stay for what you just went through."

He was such an idiot. Such a stupid idiot. He couldn't think of *any* reasons? Didn't he fucking know me by now? Didn't he have a clue who I was? Anyone who truly knew me knew I would never do this for myself. That it would only be for someone else I loved.

Goddamn him for coming in here accusing me and being cruel to me when all I needed was love and compassion, and a gentle hand to help me to the shower.

And now here he *still* was, demanding answers when he ought to be giving me understanding, when he ought to be giving me the benefit of the doubt, when he *ought* to be letting me rest until fucking tomorrow because I'd just been BURIED THE FUCK ALIVE.

But then, Sully being Sully, he just huffed out a sigh and shook his head. "Guess you're too embarrassed to just say it's for the money after all, huh?"

He backed away, disgust in his eyes. "I'm gonna go find myself a bottle of whatever the fuck will help me forget all that disturbing shit I saw tonight. You enjoy that shower."

Again, my mouth dropped open. "You can't leave the room without me. The rules—"

He gave me a cruel smirk. "The rules say *you* can't leave, cause you're a woman. Us men, kings of the universe, can wander wherever the fuck we want. And after tonight, I'm gonna go get drunk as fuck, cause, baby, it's time to forget. Forget you, forget this whole fucking fucked up fucking place."

And with that, he just... left.

He just walked out the goddamned door and *left.*

It was a familiar sight. The strong silhouette of a man's back exiting out a door without once looking back.

I'd seen the same thing as my daddy left oh so long ago.

Mama'd just died a couple months before and taking care of four daughters alone... well, that wasn't what Daddy'd signed up for, now was it?

It was so easy for them, wasn't it?

So easy to just walk out that door. No thought for the mess they left behind. The long-suffering. Daddy was fond of a bottle, too. All that easy forgetting to be found in the amber liquids. He'd take a clear liquid too, vodka was fine in a pinch, but Daddy was a whiskey man at heart.

Leaving behind a seventeen-year-old me, just on the cusp of her eighteenth birthday, to keep the bodies and spirits of my sisters and myself together.

I'd had plans. I'd wanted to go to college. I'd even had scholarships, cause God knew we were broke as hell. I'd thought maybe I could just defer one year, but that year passed by and eventually I realized I just had to let it all go. Dad wasn't coming back. Mama was buried in the ground. The girls needed a parent or the system would take them, and I'd heard too many horror stories.

And then, of course, there was Reba. Sweet, sweet Reba.

Always so like our mama.

Too much alike, it turned out.

Cause the same kidney failure that got our mama came for Reba.

It was when we got the news that Daddy left. In his note, he said he just wasn't strong enough to do it again—to watch another girl he loved go through it all.

I burned that fucking note before Reba saw it.

She was not gonna die like Mama.

Mama'd been a smoker all her life, had Type 2 Diabetes, and a host of other conditions and how fucking *dare* Dad even suggest Reba would die too?

But Reba did have to start dialysis far too young.

The truth was, she needed a new kidney and she needed it bad.

And fuck my daddy, and fuck the genes he gave me, because I wasn't a match to give my baby sister what she needed. Tanya wasn't either—maybe the youngest, LeAnn, was, but we hadn't even gotten her tested, she was too young and didn't need the burden of knowing.

The state of Georgia had one of the longest

wait-times in the nation for a new kidney. Of course it did and, of course, we had to live here. That was our luck.

But time was running out for Reba.

So, when I got a crazy invitation from a crazy man in full livery and realized it was all real and like a fairy godmother, they could grant *any wish I asked for*, even expediting my baby sister right to the front of the line for a new kidney?

Yes, you bet your ass I said sign me up. I'd do anything—*anything*—to make that happen.

And here I was.

God, I needed to scrub this dirt off me. I needed to scrub it *all* off me. I shook my head, exhausted. That old show-tune rang through my head: *I'm Gonna Wash That Man Right Outta My Hair.*

Mama used to love old movies, and she made me sit through *South Pacific* more than once. I smiled and then winced from my sore muscles.

Okay, time for a shower.

But right as I was about to shuck Sully's jacket off of me and head for the bathroom, there was a knock at the door.

For a second, my heart leapt, thinking it was Sully, come to ask for forgiveness for being such an ass, but then I frowned. Sully wouldn't knock.

I went to the door. "Who is it?"

"Mrs. Hawthorne. Portia, dear," her voice was urgent and hushed, "it's important. I need to speak to you. Please let me in."

I opened the door, hugging Sully's suit jacket even tighter around myself. "What is it?"

Mrs. Hawthorne pushed her way in and closed the door behind her. "Where's Sully?" she asked, looking around.

I crossed my arms over my chest and stared at her pointedly. "Did you have something to tell me or not?"

She looked flustered as her eyes came back to me. "Yes, dear. Your sister is here."

"What?" I rushed for the door. "Which one?"

Mrs. Hawthorne hurried to stop me before I could rush through the door and leave the room.

"She said her name was Tanya. But, honey, you can't leave without Sully."

I glared at her. "Sully left me to go off drinking somewhere. I don't give a— a *crap* about what Sullivan does or does not do right now. My sister needs me, and you will not block that door."

One of Mrs. Hawthorne's eyebrows lifted. "Be that as it may, you still can't go romping through the manor in nothing but that jacket. It might disturb your sister seeing you so disheveled. Put something else on."

Dammit, she was right. Over her shoulder, I

could see myself in the full-length mirror, and I looked—

I looked demented. My hair was crazy, my face was still streaked with dirt, and yeah, I was mostly naked.

I threw off Sully's jacket and ran for the dresser. As quickly as I could, I yanked on underclothes, leggings, socks, and a sweater. Then I ran for the bathroom and splashed water on my face, using a towel to scrub away most of the dirt.

Last, I ran a comb through my hair and tugged it up into a bun.

Then I came back to Mrs. Hawthorne. "Take me to my sister."

20

SULLY

I sat and watched the water of the pool glisten beneath the nearly full moon, trying to forget the horrors of the night. But nothing I did could get the memories of Hell out of my head. My body now shook as the shock wore off and my rage settled.

We swam tonight with blood in the water.

The Order were the sharks and there was nothing we could have done to fight them off... except leave.

Why the fuck were we still here?

Why the fuck was *she*?

Yes, she looked like the typical southern belle debutante gold digger I had grown up around, but my gut told me she was different. She had proven she was... wasn't she?

So why was the money so important to her? But actually, it couldn't be just the money or she would have taken a check from me when I offered it. She was clearly determined to not let those men win. Why? What held her here? The woman made no sense to me. One minute she was stubborn as hell, the next she was soft and in need of my help, and then she would do something else to confuse me. Why would she put herself through all of this?

And as I sat on a chair by the pool, holding a full bottle of vodka, I questioned why I was here.

Why did I expect her to leave and yet, I stayed? I simply treaded water in the bloody chum as I waited for the Order to feast on what was left of me.

Jasmine.

But was that the real reason? If I was being honest with myself, there was more to it than just inheriting the family business for the sake of my sister.

I didn't want the men of the Order to be able to break me either. I refused to let them win just as Portia did.

Staring at the vodka bottle, I also asked myself why I was still sober. I hadn't even taken a sip. Why the fuck not?

Because of *her.*

She didn't want me to drink.

And I cared about what she wanted... dammit I cared a lot.

"Sully!" I heard Mrs. H call as she walked out to join me at the pool. The woman looked frazzled, but I seemed to have been doing that to her a lot lately. "What are you doing out here?"

"I just needed some time to think," I said, placing the untouched booze bottle on the table beside me.

"You left that poor girl when she needed you the most!" Mrs. H approached me and stood with her hands on her hips and a look of judgment painted on her face.

"She doesn't need anyone," I said. "She's strong."

"Damn straight she's strong, stronger than you even know. But that doesn't give you an excuse to throw a fit like a child and leave her alone in that room."

"She'll be fine," I mumbled, waiting for Mrs. H's wrath to end. I had learned as a young boy to take your lumps from the woman, and then she'd forgive, she'd love, and she'd send us on our way.

I glanced up at Mrs. H and took in her appearance. Standing with the lit-up pool behind her made me realize that she must have been a very beautiful woman in her youth—and still was. Yes, she was an older lady now, but not frail. Each wrinkle on her face made her seem wiser and worldly. She hadn't changed one bit since I was young when it came to her temper, and her stead-fast personality actually filled me with comfort even as she stood furious before me.

"You know what, Sullivan VanDoren, you can be a real son of a bitch sometimes."

I inhaled deeply. Here came the tongue lashing.

"Your daddy is rolling in his grave over how you've conducted yourself since arriving at the Oleander."

"Well, thank the almighty for that," I said under my breath but instantly regretted saying the words when Mrs. H reached out and smacked me upside the head.

"Don't you speak like that. You may have Daddy issues, young man, but that doesn't mean your father was the devil."

"He was an asshole."

"Maybe," she said. "I might agree with you that he lost his way as time went on. Many of the men in the Order have. But I will tell you one thing... at least your father *lost* his way. You, on the other hand, have yet to find a way to lose." She took a deep breath, her chest rising, before she continued. "I know you've done everything you can to not be like him."

"I would rather die than be like that man," I spat.

"But you're more like him than you know."

"Mrs. H, I love you, but I'm not going to sit here and let you insult me."

She took a step closer to me, which would have made it difficult for me to get off the chair without pushing her out of my way. So, seated I stayed.

"I'm not insulting you if it's the truth, sonny. And do you think you're the first VanDoren to leave Georgia to go find yourself?" When I didn't answer, she continued on. "Well, you aren't. Your father did the same thing when he was young too. He tried to run just like you but returned for the same reasons. Your heritage is a strong pull. The ghosts of your ancestors beckon, and you have no choice but to come calling."

Her information about my father was news to me, but that didn't change anything.

"You are a VanDoren. You have duties and responsibilities. You have your mother—"

"I'm not here for my mother," I cut in. "She'll do just fine without my help. She has plenty of money and pearls and whatever other rich-bitch shit all those Southern socialites need."

"Stop, young man!" she snapped. "Do you hear yourself? You sound like a spoiled brat. You may not like your Southern roots, but don't you dare start attacking and judging those who do." She pointed to the manor. "You aren't better than them. You can keep telling yourself you are, but you aren't. In fact, you are quite the arsehole right now if you want my honesty."

I glanced at the vodka bottle and considered taking a swig from it right then but feared I could give the old woman a stroke. "Call me whatever you want. And you're right. I am an *arsehole*. We all are, which is why I left to begin with. I'm trying to be a better man, but I can't do it here."

"Running does not make you a better man. Hiding from what made you, and the people who love you is not the way. You run, you drink, you resist everything and everyone, and all it does is hurt you. Not better you."

"Fine. Your message is heard loud and clear. Are we done yet?"

"I'm half tempted to go find a broom and beat you silly, young man. Someone clearly has to."

I closed my eyes and leaned back in my chair. "What is it you expect from me? What more can I do? I'm sitting here in this manor even though I don't want to. I'm doing this for Jasmine even though I fear the business will turn her into someone like my father. I'm trying to be the bigger man."

"Yes, Jasmine. Think about that poor child

when you make your impulsive decisions. You may hate your roots, but don't force those thoughts upon her. She may be proud of them. She may want to see them grow and thrive rather than rot in the dirt like you."

I opened my eyes and made direct contact with hers. "I get it. Okay? I get it."

Mrs. H extended a bony finger at me. "It's time you grow up, Sully. And I could stand here and lecture you all day, but you need to go after Portia and help bring her back here before you both get caught by the Order and fail the Initiation."

"Wait... What?" I said, standing to my feet which made Mrs. H take a few steps back. "Did Portia leave the Oleander?"

Mrs. H nodded. "Which you'd know if you weren't out here wallowing."

Even though my heart sank to my gut, I couldn't say I blamed her. "I guess it's about time she did," I said.

But damn... we were so close. Our 109 days were almost over, and it did seem like a fucking shame that we went through all of those shitty Trials to walk away empty handed. But I wouldn't hold us failing against Portia either.

Hell... she should have left the manor screaming from the first night.

"She's not running from the Initiation," Mrs. H said. "She's running to be with her sister."

"Her sister?"

"Yes..." Mrs. H tilted her head and studied my face. "Didn't she tell you about her sister?"

"No... what? Why would she leave for her sister?"

Mrs. H shook her head. "That girl... I told her —" she refocused her attention back on me and said, "She's at the hospital. Her sister is extremely sick. Portia needs you right now. But she needs a man, not a boy."

Sick?

Mrs. H extended her hand and gripped my arm softly. "I know you. I know the man you are and the demons you're fighting. But right now, that sweet girl needs your strength and support. It's time you open your eyes and see past the darkness you have blanketed everything and everyone in. Make the VanDoren name one to be respected. I know you can."

"What's wrong with her sister? Why is she in the hospital?" My head swirled and my body tensed. I racked my brain for any mention of a sister being sick and couldn't remember even the slightest clue. Why would Portia not tell me this?

"It's not my story to tell," Mrs. H said. "But she's at St. Josephs right now."

As I got ready to run to my truck that I hadn't touched in almost 109 days, I paused. "Does the Order know she's left yet?"

Mrs. H shook her head. "Not yet. I haven't, nor will I, say a word. But you know them..."

I sighed realizing we could have very well gone through this entire Initiation only to have it ruined tonight. They had a way of knowing everything. But fuck that. Who cares? It wasn't about them right now. It wasn't about The Order of the Silver Ghost. It wasn't about me. It wasn't about my demons with my father and my history. It wasn't about everything I hated.

No. It was about someone I loved. Loved.

It was about Portia Collins.

She was all that mattered right now.

21

PORTIA

I all but leapt out of the car once I parked at the hospital. I drove. No way I was trusting Tanya with our ancient Toyota Prius on the dark roads around Darlington at night. The last thing we needed was to hit a deer when Reba needed us.

But screw the speed limit. Tanya was a freaking expert at talking and hair-flipping her way out of speeding tickets, and God could only be so cruel to one family, couldn't he?

Rebs needed me and I would get to her, come hell or high water.

I'd grilled Tanya the whole drive about her condition, but hadn't gotten much other than, "She's really sick," out of her. Reba had apparently had another UTI, a *big* problem for someone in the end stages of renal failure, and

Tanya had gotten her to the hospital "just in time".

Whatever the fuck that meant. But it was also bad enough to come and get me when we all knew why I was there.

And I was fucking terrified that Tanya had only come and gotten me so I'd have a chance to say goodbye.

The very thought of *ever* saying goodbye to my baby sister put a fire in my belly that had me now sprinting across the parking lot. I ran into the lobby and demanded, "I need to see Reba Collins."

"I know what room she's in. LeAnn texted me," Tanya said from behind me, holding up her phone. Probably a good thing because the lady behind the intake desk frankly looked afraid of me, or like she was about two seconds away from calling for backup.

I ignored her and turned to Tanya. "Let's go. Where is she?"

Tanya asked for directions, something I was in no mood to do, and then we hurried down the hallways and up the elevator to the second floor and down even more hallways.

"Come on, baby, come on, baby," I kept whispering under my breath. "Come on, baby girl. You're gonna be just fine." She had to be. She'd come this far. We'd all come this far. She'd be fine.

We finally came to a lobby and LeAnn jumped up from a chair. Her normally perfect make-up was blotchy and smeared. She'd obviously been crying. She ran towards us and flung her arms around me.

"Where have you *been*?" she cried even as she squeezed me. "Beba is so sick. And you ran away just like Daddy." LeAnn's pet name for Reba had been Beba ever since she was little and couldn't pronounce her R's right. The name had stuck ever since.

Gut punch. Of course Tanya and I hadn't told her where I was really going or what I was doing. But I had told her I was going for Reba. I combed my fingers through LeAnn's hair as I clutched her to me, tears finally falling down my own cheeks. "You know I was gone to try to get Reba her new kidney."

LeAnn pulled back from me, eyes hopeful. "Did you get it? She needs it, Porsche. She needs it now or it might not matter."

Double gut punch. I shook my head, my bottom lip trembling. After tonight, leaving the premises like this... no, there was no way. I'd lost my chance. I'd lost Reba her chance at a kidney.

It had all been for nothing.

LeAnn made a noise of grief and anger and I pulled her close to me. She resisted for a long moment but finally gave in. She didn't hug me back, but at least she let me hug her. I needed it even if she was angry at me right now for failing her. For failing all of them.

"Tell me. How is she?" I asked. "Did they let you see her?"

LeAnn pulled back, all the way away from me and crossed her arms over her chest. She dropped her gaze to the floor, her hair falling and shielding her features from me. Still, I heard her murmur, "It's bad."

Goddammit, why did everyone keep saying that but not giving me any more details?

But just then, a nurse came out. I hurried over. "I'm the oldest sister of Reba Collins. Please, I need to know her condition. What's happening with her? Is there a doctor I can speak to about her condition?"

A look of sympathy passed over the woman's face. "I'll get Dr. Reynard for you. Just one moment."

I nodded and let her continue on her way. She gave some papers to another person in the waiting room then disappeared back behind the door. I paced and bit at my fingernails for the next ten minutes until a middle-aged woman emerged.

I hurried over to her. "Dr. Reynard?" I asked hopefully. "I'm Reba's oldest sister."

She gave a soft, kindly smile. "She was asking for you earlier, but she's asleep now."

Ten thousandth gut punch. She'd been in pain, so sick, and asking for me—and I wasn't there. I'd been out trying to catch a hail-Mary pass and failing spectacularly.

"How is she?"

Dr. Reynard's face clouded. "Not so good. She's in the final stages of renal failure. Getting another UTI put stress on her renal system that it just couldn't handle."

"What the hell does that mean?" I asked sharply. Then I winced. "Shit, I'm sorry." Then realized I'd just cussed again. "I'm sorry. So, does she finally get moved to the front of the list? Can she get a transplant?"

And then came *The Look*.

The same fucking look I'd seen on a hundred doctors' faces—first when my mom was dying and then later when Reba was a teenager and we found out she had the same kidney disease Mama finally died of.

The Look that said, oh so sorry, the doctor felt bad, but there was Nothing They Could Do.

I started shaking my head. "No," I said. I took the doctor's forearm and steered us away from my sisters, to the corner of the room. "No. My sister deserves that kidney. She deserves to be at the front of the list. Tanya didn't tell me much, but she told me Reba *collapsed*. She f— She freaking collapsed. My mom *died* of this. I cannot go tell those girls over there that they're going to lose their sister, too. Don't you dare make me go tell them that. You're a doctor. Fix my sister!"

Dr. Reynard looked at me more compassionately than most doctors bothered with. And I got it, I really did. She was working a night shift in a regional hospital in Nowheresfuck, Georgia. Still, *still*. If she wouldn't help me, who the fuck would?

"It's still possible the antibiotics will kick in and she'll recover from the UTI, and I'll do everything I can to see if I can bump up her priority status on the list, but there are very strict guidelines and simply so many people in need, plus so few donors—"

I turned away from her, sick to death of the words I'd heard a thousand times before.

Just in time to see Sully running into the waiting room, his heavy footfalls echoing even as he came to a stop, looking around.

His eyes landed on me about three point two seconds after I'd seen him.

He'd come.

He'd left the Oleander and risked everything

he'd stayed for, whatever the hell had kept him there enduring all that he hated, he'd left it all.

For me.

I fled across the room and flung myself into his arms.

They wouldn't let me in to see Reba all night. All excruciating night long I had to wait to see my beautiful baby sister.

The only way I survived it was Sully.

Once he had me in his arms, he didn't let go. He kept hold of me in some way, even if it was grasping my hand in his while I haltingly introduced him to Tanya and LeAnn. They were curious —Tanya looked outright suspicious of him in his fancy tux the Elders had given him—good Lord, had that only been earlier tonight when he'd tromped so confidently down those stairs naked by my side? It felt like a lifetime ago.

So yeah, Tanya all but glared at him all night as he stayed by my side. LeAnn looked at him like he was a knight in shining armor come to save us.

She'd watched too much old school Disney growing up—completely all my fault.

I knew better. Sully couldn't save Reba any more than I could.

But he'd done what he could—he'd come. He'd sacrificed whatever it was that being in The Order of the Silver Ghost had meant to him.

He was here.

For me.

I even managed the impossible. For about an hour, I fell asleep against his chest while we waited for the morning visiting hours.

And when I woke up, it was to stare up into the most incredible brown eyes. The morning sun was finally streaming through the window, and his eyes were glowing translucent with the light.

For once he didn't look troubled. For once he didn't look angry.

He was watching me intently, and he looked full of... some emotion I couldn't name. I'd never seen it on his face before.

But as my eyes blinked him into focus, he lifted one of his big, brutal hands and caressed my face with the gentlest touch. So gentle it sent a shiver throughout my entire body.

"Why didn't you tell me, beautiful?" he whispered, a deep, tender bass to his voice.

I answered as honestly as I could. "You never asked, not really. You just assumed."

His eyes closed briefly, and his head dropped before he nodded. Then he pulled me close and kissed me on the forehead. So, so sweetly. I'd never felt his lush lips so soft before.

It felt wrong to feel so good in his arms when my sister, my sister—

A sob caught in my chest.

Sully pulled me in tighter. "It's okay, babe. You can tell me now." I looked over his shoulders for my sisters as I shook my head. I had to keep it together for them.

"While you were sleeping, I told Tanya to take LeAnn home for a while," he said into my hair.

I pulled back, mostly in shock. "And she listened to you?"

Sully smirked, so stunning, so perfect. "Turns out you Collins girls are a stubborn bunch. She did warn me she'd cut off my balls if I hurt you first. But LeAnn needed a break, so she gave in."

I smiled wanly. It sounded like Tanya. And then my lip trembled again, and I couldn't hold it back anymore.

I dug my face into his shoulder and sobbed. "Reba," I wailed into his shoulder. "She's only twenty years old. She hasn't even lived yet! I was supposed to get her a kidney from the Order but I even screwed *that* up."

Sully didn't hush me or tell me to stop crying. He just nodded and asked me more about it. Turned out he could be a really good listener when he wanted to be. He listened to how I'd always been Mom after Mama died and Daddy ran off. How sometimes it all got to be so much *I'd* dreamed about running off in my worst moments. But Reba was the best of us and the least deserving of the shit serving life had dealt her.

And somehow Sully listened and didn't do the thing I hated when guys did—he didn't offer suggestions on how to fix it or immediately try to give ten different ways he would have done things differently.

He just... listened.

And then, after I was all talked out and he was still holding me, he told me about *his* sister.

Turned out we'd always had so much more in common than we'd ever imagined.

"Funny how much we are alike even though we are also very different. I had a dad my entire life. He didn't run out on us, well, at least not the same way yours did on you. But my father worked all the time, and when he wasn't working, he was at the Oleander. The Order of the Silver Ghost meant more to him than my mother, my sister Jasmine and myself combined."

"I'm sure that had to be hard," I said.

"It was what it was. But I sure as hell wanted to get away from it all as soon as I could. And I did. I literally went West until I reached the sea and couldn't get any further. California was my sanctuary, but even miles apart couldn't keep me from this shit. He died, and I had to return."

"Why?" I asked. "I get the feeling you hated your father. So why did you feel the need to come back for him?"

"I didn't come back for him, or his funeral." He released a deep breath. "Yes, I hated my father. He was a selfish son of a bitch who cared about himself and his prestige only. Nothing I, or my sister did, was good enough.

"He never hit us or anything, but I would have taken a physical beating over the verbal one we got each day he blessed us with his occasional presence. I came back to offer support for my sister, and I suppose if I was being honest with myself... I even came back for my mother in some sick way."

He shook his head. "My mother wasn't much better than my father. She was more concerned with parties and her charities than her own children. Both my parents were self-absorbed and did very little in raising us. You can thank the constant flow of nannies for my lovely personality." A small smile quirked his lips. "But my sister was different. Jasmine had a pure heart, her love for me was the only genuine love I ever truly felt growing up and even now. She was like me. She didn't ask to be born into this silver spoon-fed nightmare, nor did I."

"It's better than poverty. Trust me on that."

He nodded. "Maybe. I wouldn't know. But I'll tell you this. I hate money. I hate what it does to people. I hate the thirst, materialistic need, and all-consuming greed that surrounded me my entire life."

"Then why did you even want to try to become part of the Order?"

"For my sister. I need to complete the Trials in order to get the family business. VanDoren Enterprises does not automatically get passed down to me. It's in my father's will. A member of the Order must own the business. I have to become a member or lose it all."

I watched how even talking about this bothered him. His jaw locked; his eyes seemed to darken with every word. "I don't understand. You just said you hated all that. So why would you want the family business?"

"I don't want it. But my sister does. And classic fucked up Order style prevents her from inheriting it at all. I'm doing this for her. Only for her."

"Miss Collins?" I looked up and then jumped to my feet when I saw the nice nurse from last night.

"Yes?"

"I'm just getting off shift. But Dr. Reynard asked me to let you in a little early to see your sister since you've been waiting all night. She's awake now."

"Thank you!"

I grabbed Sully's hand and all but dragged him through the door she was holding open. The rest of the waiting room was empty.

I was still reeling from all he'd told me.

He'd stayed and endured all those horrific Trials for love of a sister too. Family meant something to him. A huge part of his life had been defined by his father's betrayal and abandonment —it was still abandonment even if it had been in a different form than my father's. Even more insidious maybe, because he was still there all the time but making the active choice every day for work and the Order over his family waiting for him at home. Hurting Sully as deeply as my father had hurt me.

It was only a little further to Reba's room. I did leave Sully outside since I didn't want to have to explain him to Reba when the focus needed to be on her, but just knowing he was nearby was a huge comfort. Not that I wanted to explore that thought too much. But he'd seriously shown up for me last night, and after everything we'd been through together...

I rounded the corner and my mouth dropped open when I saw Reba.

"Beba," I cried, using LeAnn's pet name for her. I rushed to the bed and sat on the edge beside her tiny, wan little body.

What the *hell* had happened since I left just three months ago?

She was skin and fucking bones.

I grabbed her hand and it was ice cold to the touch. I immediately started chafing it back and forth to warm it up.

"Hey, babe," I said, trying to infuse my voice with as much warmth as possible. She didn't need to know how crazy freaked out I was seeing her like this.

Her eyes were sunken, her lips dry, her skin... She looked like she was...

She looked like she was dying.

I gripped her hand like I could send some of my own life force into her limp body.

She opened her mouth like she was trying to say hi or say my name but no words came out.

I shook my head. "No, babe. It's fine. Don't even

try to talk. I heard you had a little mishap and your legs gave out on you. Not cool, legs."

I shook my finger at her legs, then smiled back at her. "But big sis is here now. I'll fix everything, like always."

But she just looked at me with this wisdom like, like— Like she didn't believe me.

Like I didn't know what I was talking about.

Like I was the child and she was the grown-up who understood grown-up realities like death and dying while I was still a little baby kick-boxing at shadows I had no hope of winning against or even comprehending.

I just shook my head. "No, Rebs. No."

She smiled the tiniest little smile.

And then her eyes went wide with shock and what looked like excruciating pain. A thin, reedy wail of pain came out of her throat and all the machines hooked up to her started going haywire.

"Reba. Reba!" I shouted.

But she couldn't answer. Her eyes had rolled back in her head.

I ran for the door, screaming, "Nurse! Doctor! *Doctor!*"

23

SULLY

The hospital walls seemed to be closing in on us, the shadows of the dead haunting the hallways reminding us that not everyone leaves this building alive.

Portia's sister was dying and there was absolutely nothing I could do to help. Portia had been so dazed and upset when the doctor had talked to us about what was wrong with her sister—recurrent UTIs because of her being in the last stages of renal disease leading to a rare complication, something something. Long story short—if she didn't get that new kidney, she was gonna die.

For the first time in my life, I wished I was my father.

My father had power. Wealth. Massive strings he could pull.

He'd be able to save Portia's sister.

He'd be able to make it right.

But because I had been so damn stubborn and had resisted every leg up that had been offered to me, I didn't even know where to start in trying to get that poor girl a kidney. I couldn't just make a few phone calls and get it done.

I was helpless.

God, I wish I was like my father.

My eyes were closed, but I wasn't asleep. I had been up all night as Portia slept on my shoulder between her constant getting up and asking for updates on her sister. Exhaustion had set in, but I worried that if I fell asleep, I wouldn't be there if she needed me. I wasn't going to leave her for even a second.

I may not be able to give her sister a kidney, but I sure as hell could give all of me to Portia.

A tap on the shoulder that Portia wasn't leaned up against had me opening my eyes startled.

It was Montgomery Kingston.

I blinked a few times to make sure it was indeed a reality and not some overly tired and twisted dream, but when I saw my old friend's concerned face, and his head motioning for me to come speak to him, I knew this nightmare was indeed a reality.

The Order had found me.

They knew Portia and I had left... all was lost.

I wasn't sure how to move without waking Portia, but she made it an easy decision when she lifted her head and looked at Montgomery.

"They know we left?" she asked Montgomery.

He nodded. "They do."

"It was an emergency," I said.

Montgomery nodded sadly and then looked at Portia with deep sympathy written across every inch of his face and in the depths of his eyes. "I'm sorry about your sister. When The Order of the Silver Ghost heard... well, when I heard... anyway, I'm really sorry."

She nodded and then stood. She stretched her body and rolled the kinks out of her neck. "I should go check on Reba and see if there's any updates," she said.

I reached for her hand and squeezed it, silently telling her I was there for her if she needed me.

When she left the waiting room, I spun my attention to Montgomery. "So, are you here to tell me that we lost the Initiation? Did they send you to do the dirty work?"

"I wanted it to be me," Montgomery said. "And no, you haven't officially failed it yet. They're calling for both of you to return to the Oleander to face the music."

"Why bother?" I rubbed the sleep out of my

eyes. "Frankly, I couldn't care less if I ever step foot in that house ever again."

"You both were nearly done with the Trials. Don't you want to see if they'll make an exception, considering the reason you both left?"

"I've never known the Elders to be merciful or caring in any way. Rules are rules," I said. "You know this as much as I do."

"Don't admit defeat," Montgomery said as he took the empty seat beside me. "I know why you were doing it. I also now know why Portia was."

"A kidney," I said. "She was doing it to save her sister's life."

I shook my head, feeling so shallow and low. My reason, and every person's reason for doing the Initiation seemed so small in comparison. The Order of the Silver Ghost were the kingmakers and the dreammakers, and they had the power to grant Portia her wish. But now... well, it didn't really matter now. What was done was done.

"How's her sister doing?" Montgomery asked in a soft voice.

"Awful. Dying. She's in a lot of pain, and the staff are trying to do everything they can to make her comfortable, but it's not pretty. Portia's sisters went to get some sleep which is good. But Reba's going downhill fast."

"And they can't get her a kidney?"

"Not fast enough. No." I leaned forward with my elbows on my legs and ran my hand through my hair. I was pretty sure I looked like a hot mess. It was my first time spending hours upon hours in a hospital, but I had no intention of leaving without Portia.

"I tried to make all the calls I could." I shook my head. "I even went to the Administration and did what I swore I would never do in my life. I tried to use the VanDoren name to get what I wanted. It was useless."

"The Order can get that kidney or they wouldn't have granted Portia's request before she started the Trials," Montgomery said.

"Right, well we clearly fucked that up. I seriously doubt they'll just hand me an ice cooler with a kidney in it as a consolation prize for failing the Initiation."

"You didn't fail. You disqualified," Montgomery said. "And we don't even know that. They're asking for you both to return and address this."

"I'm not leaving Portia," I said. "Not even an option right now. And Portia isn't going to leave her sister, so there's—"

"We'll go," Portia interrupted as she entered the waiting room. "Reba's sleeping and my sisters are on their way here again." She looked at me. "We need to go face this. Probably nothing will come out of it... but if there's any chance for that kidney... if they have any compassion at all..."

Her tear-filled eyes came to mine. I wasn't sure how to tell her I didn't think the Order knew what the word *compassion* meant. It wasn't in their fucking dictionary.

I stood up and put my arms around her and whispered into her ear, "The Order. The Initiation. It's all noise. Ignore it."

"We can't," she said as she pulled away from my embrace but took my hand in hers. "I made a commitment. You did too. Pretending they don't exist, doesn't make this disappear. We have to go. We have to *try*." Her voice broke on the last word.

And I saw then exactly why this woman had subjected herself to every humiliating and degrading and painful Trial the Order had asked of her. She would truly do *anything* for her family. Even walk back to the Lion's Den with her head held high and beg.

I took a deep breath and looked at Montgomery. "Call them up. We'll head back now."

As I drove us back to the Oleander, I finally broke the long silence between us. "I promise you that once we leave here, I won't stop until I find a way to get Reba that kidney. I'll see if I can get Montgomery or other friends to help. I might not have the strength of the Order, but I won't give up."

She continued to stare out the window at the rows of oak trees passing by. "The waiting list is long. Really long."

"I know," I said. "But I promise you that I'll fight. I won't just accept no."

She sighed and closed her eyes. Her shoulders sunk and her body seemed so small and fragile against the leather of the seat. If I could have taken her into my arms right then and there, I'm not sure I would have ever let her go.

As we pulled up to the manor, I tried to ignore the sick feeling in my stomach. I knew what I had to do, and it was going to test every part of my being. "Are you sure you want to go in there?"

She opened her eyes and nodded. "Nothing we can do but offer our truth."

Our truth.

Mrs. H met us at the door. She examined Portia's face and then said, "Whatever happens in there, I want you to know what you did was right." She looked at me. "It took courage, and I'm very proud of the both of you."

She led us to the white ballroom where the Elders sat in their silver cloaks with canes in hand behind a long table. The rest of the members flanked the walls, and I knew what would come next.

Judgment.

The Final Ceremony.

"Sully VanDoren. Portia Collins. You both have failed to reach the 109 days to complete the Trials of Initiation," one of the Elders announced as he stood and struck his cane hard against the floor as a signal that the ceremony had begun.

109. The address of the Oleander, 109 Oleander Lane. Simple upon first reflection, but some numerologist back in the beginning had a field day with it—100 plus 9. 9 being 3x3, and 3 being the number of divinity, well, it was perfect. To pass through 109 days of Trials at the Oleander Manor was to achieve a kind of divinity among their ranks, and be ushered into the brotherhood, the gods of men, modern day kings of empires.

In other words—Such. Utter. Bullshit.

"Because of your breach of our terms about leaving the Oleander, the Order has called for the Final Ceremony to occur now."

The elder sitting on the far right of the table asked, "Sullivan VanDoren, please state to us why you broke the rule of The Order of the Silver Ghost and left the manor."

The fuckers knew the answer.

The old me would have spoken those words out loud. I would have been an asshole. I would have pushed. I would have called names. I would have fought for me... instead of fighting for Portia... for us.

But it was now time I bite my tongue and grow the fuck up. It was time. It was long past time.

"There was a family emergency, and Portia needed to be with her sister. The decision was not made lightly, but we both didn't feel we had a choice," I said calmly. "The Order stands for loyalty, and if one cannot demonstrate loyalty for one's family, how can they hope to do so for the Order?"

The elder who first spoke said, "Loyalty to the Order comes first *before* loyalty to any outside familial connections. You know better. Is there any opposition by any of the Elders as to why we should not disqualify the two?"

"I oppose," Montgomery said as he took a step toward the Elders. "I know I'm not an elder, but I am now a member of the Order. I feel that this should not only be an elder decision. I feel that every member should have a say in the fate of Mr. VanDoren and Portia Collins. A vote should be cast. We should all have a say."

I reached out and took Portia's clammy hand in mine. There was nothing either of us could do but stand before them and hope that our chances weren't completely over. Could Montgomery help us?

Unlikely.

But maybe...

One of the Elders spoke. "It specifically states in our bylaws that no recruit going through the initiation may leave the manor for *any* reason. Due to his breach, he can no longer claim his stake in the VanDoren business nor join our order. The belle can no longer claim her dream."

Montgomery seemed unfazed by the Elders. "I understand that there are rules. But both Sully and Portia have completed each Trial without fail. They were far from easy, and both did each one with the courage and respect of the process that the Order requires. I believe they deserve to have what they came here for."

Mr. Sinclair—an Elder I knew was not a fan of me even though I was a very good friend of his son Walker—pounded his cane against the ground to stop the back-and-forth discussion. "Our bloodlines represent respect, prestige, and wealth. We are the elite, and you, Sullivan VanDoren, have resisted us and what we stand for from the minute you walked through the door of the Oleander. You do not value our rules, nor do you respect what The Order of the Silver Ghost is all about. For you to stand there and expect us to have mercy on you and the belle..." he narrowed his eyes and leaned in. "Tell us why we should."

I scanned the Elders looking for some kind of clue as to what they wanted to hear, but the faces of the men remained emotionless. I couldn't read them, but I could see that Walker's dad wanted me to plead my case.

Plead... beg... hell, I would get down on my knees for this if I had to.

So that is exactly what I did.

Releasing Portia's hand, I took a few steps closer to where the Elders sat. I got down on my knees and bowed my head, pausing so the full effect could sink in for each man deciding my fate.

"I admit that I have not respected the Order up to this point. I have not respected the VanDoren name. In fact, I have tried to resist it in every single way. But I am here, on my knees, *begging* you all to have mercy on the woman behind me. We can't fail the Initiation because an innocent woman will die if we do. The belle's wish that would be granted is to have the Order secure a kidney for her dying sister. We only left the Order because her sister is very close to dying, not because of my lack of respect for the Order."

I lifted my gaze from the floor so that I could look each elder in the eye. "Please. I am a VanDoren. My father sat among you. He was your friend, your brother, your colleague. You respected him." I set my stare on Walker's dad. "And though you don't respect me, I ask you for the sake of my father to grant his son lenience. Can you do it for him? For the VanDoren name. Please."

And there it was. I was a VanDoren and using the power of that name to get what I needed. I was using my father to help me when I never thought I would allow it. But I needed him. Maybe not in life, but I needed him now in death. I needed my heritage. I needed my ancestry. I needed what my dad had worked so hard to build.

I suppose I could have always tried to use my name for good rather than run and hide from it. I suppose I could have been a man and not tried to fight it but embrace it instead.

Being a VanDoren didn't need to be a curse. It was a name I could be proud of.

Maybe it was too late, but I had to try.

"My name is Sullivan VanDoren. It is my birthright to be a member of The Order of the Silver Ghost. I respectfully ask the Order to grant me that right."

The first elder who had beat his cane to start the ceremony did so again. Loud beats of wood against marble caused reverberations to run up my knees as I remained in a position of submission and humility.

"Mr. VanDoren, please leave the ballroom with your belle so we can discuss the matter brought before us." He hit the cane again as the period to his request.

Realizing I had been holding my breath, I released it and stood. I cast a glance at Montgomery who gave me a reassuring nod before I approached Portia who stood motionless with tears in her eyes.

I placed my hand on her lower back and guided her out of the ballroom as was expected.

"All we can do is wait," I said.

"You... you... did that for me?" she said as a single tear ran down her cheek. "You got down on your knees for me in front of those men you hate. You fought for us. You—"

I silenced her with a kiss, firm and possessive. I needed her touch just as much as I was sure she needed mine. Pulling away, I swiped at the tears that continued to fall from her bright blue eyes. "There isn't anything I wouldn't do for you. For your sister. And from this moment on I'll be the warrior by your side even if that means me dropping my sword."

She wrapped her arms around me and pressed her face into my neck. In the softest mumble, I heard words that I never knew would mean so much to me. "You aren't the man I expected, Sully VanDoren. I can't ever thank you enough. What you did for me in there. What you said... I know it wasn't easy."

"No, it wasn't. Fucking made me sick. But if it makes them take pause and not instantly fail us, then I would kiss each of their feet if I had to. I would crawl across glass to get there. I would do anything."

I took a piece of her hair hanging on her face and caressed it behind her ear. "I know I've not been a man you can count on. At least not in here. But I'm going to change that. With love comes a responsibility I will never run from. I'm here. I'm here for you. I won't hide. I won't try to escape. I'm here."

We didn't have long to stand there and process our declarations of love because the banging of canes and the door opening to the ballroom made it very clear that a decision had been made.

"No matter what, we're in this together," I said as I led us both back into the ballroom.

I found Montgomery in the sea of bodies, but he wouldn't look me in the eyes.

Something was wrong. This wasn't going to be good.

Feeling as if I needed to still be on my knees, I took my spot before them and got down to the floor. Portia joined me, and though I don't think the Order would ever expect a belle to plead beside a recruit, it showed just how much we both hoped for their mercy.

Mr. Sinclair spoke loudly. "The Order of the Silver Ghost have taken a vote as Montgomery Kingston suggested. It was decided that one of you can pass the Initiation. But just one."

He then directed his attention toward Portia, then at me. "Sullivan VanDoren, we leave the decision up to you. You can be the one to pass. You can be the one to take over the VanDoren business as your father had intended, and you can become a member of The Order of the Silver Ghost. *Or* Portia Collins can be the one to complete the Initiation. Her request was a kidney which the Order is prepared to grant today. The arrangements can be made immediately."

My heart stopped and head spun.

One choice. Only one choice.

No VanDoren Enterprises. Nothing to pass to Jasmine. All my time being here and my goal would not be met if I chose the kidney for Portia's sister.

We would not win together.

One loser. One winner.

Mr. Sinclair continued. "To reiterate, you can only have one option. So what will it be? Will the Order be a kingmaker or a dreammaker?"

24

My mouth dropped open in shock. That wasn't fair! It had been a family emergency. My sister was dying. Didn't these bastards have a drop of compassion in their cold, soulless hearts—

"Give Portia her sister's kidney," Sully said in a loud, booming voice. "I forfeit my right to my father's company."

My mouth dropped open and I spun to him. "Sully, no! It's your heritage. You just told me how important it is to your family. Your mom. Your *sister*."

Sully just shook his head and reached up and cupped my face. "It's not life and death, baby. And you don't know it yet, but I'm really fucking motivated when I want to be. I'll make sure Mom and Jasmine are taken care of."

Mr. Sinclair interrupted anything else Sully might have been about to say. "It has been decided. Ms. Collins, your wish will be granted immediately. A kidney is ready and will be transported to St. Mary's Hospital within the hour."

My legs buckled but Sully caught me before I hit the ground. Was it real? It couldn't be real. After all this time...

"Now exit the manor while we discuss the terms of sale of VanDoren Enterprises," Mr. Sinclair continued. "Since Sullivan will not be assuming the helm, it will now be up for auction to the members."

If Sully was blindsided by this move, he didn't show it. He just tugged my arm around his waist and supported me as I walked on wobbly legs towards the door of the ballroom, then through the foyer, then down the steps onto the front drive.

I blinked unsteadily in the morning light. "Were they serious?"

"The Order doesn't make promises they can't keep. Your sister will have that kidney within the hour."

That sent a wash of relief and warmth through me. Reba could really be okay. These crazy, powerful, sadistic bastards really could do miracles. I shook my head in disbelief.

But then I looked back at Sully, stricken again when I remembered what he'd given up for me. "But, Sully, your company!"

He shrugged, like it wasn't a big deal. "It was my father's company, not mine. It was never mine."

I wasn't going to let him off that easy. "But it could have been. It was yours by rights. And your sister's. They have no right to think they can just auction it off—"

Sully reached out and gently took my hands, squeezing them. "They have every right. This was my father's world and he loved it. He loved the Order and their power and prestige more than anything. More than his own family, I thought sometimes. I'm sure the old bastard is glancing up from Hell and nodding in approval at everything they're doing."

I squeezed Sully's hand harder. He looked outwards, above my head at the avenue of oaks lining the long driveway. Their leaves were browned by winter. We had similar oaks near where I lived and they'd briefly drop their leaves right before new ones grew in the spring, not true evergreens. But ever symbols of majesty and witness bearers of the ages. A truth echoed by Sully's next words.

"And today I got a glimpse of at least maybe why he did a little bit of what he did. Supporting his family and always giving us the best was important to him. He fought hard to grow his empire into what it was at its peak. Drove himself into an early grave doing it, but it can't be said the man didn't have ambition."

Watching Sully's conflicted features as he spoke about his father made me want to wrap my arms around him. And my legs. I wanted to wrap my entire body around him and comfort him and make everything better.

I was so sorry for the deep-down ache his father being so busy and never having time for him had obviously caused. I wanted to go back in time and shake the man and tell him, "Don't you see what an amazing son you have? Wake up! He's amazing! Appreciate him and both of y'all learn to love each other better while you have time! The leaves will fall and your time will be through and it will be too late!"

But there weren't any time machines, of course. And all we could do was love each other now and soothe away the pain our parents had inflicted on us. Rub ointment on each other's scars so they healed over just like my brand was doing.

"You know I love you, right?" Sully said, out of the blue.

I choked a little on my tongue, but finally managed to stutter, "W-what?"

He looked down at me and smirked. "You love me, too. You probably fell in love with me first."

I smacked him on the chest. "Did not!" But then I immediately followed it up with a haughty, "Obviously *you* fell in love with *me* first. You couldn't keep your hands off me."

He laughed, a big, booming laugh that lit me up all the way down to my toes. *He said he loves me!* It wouldn't stop pinging around my brain like a little electric shock. *He loves me!*

"Baby, I hate to educate you in the ways of men, but that does not always equal love."

I smacked him on the chest again for that one. Hard. And arched an eyebrow at him. "Well, if that's the way you feel, maybe I won't be throwing this body around so freely with you in the future."

I started to pull back from him, but he wrapped his arms around my waist and pulled me back so that I was flush against his pelvis, and suddenly his eyes were serious.

"No, gorgeous, don't say that." His eyes searched mine. "And I'm still waiting for you to say it back."

I swallowed; my mouth suddenly gone dry. But he'd been courageous, so courageous, and I could be, too. "I love you."

Simple, straight, and to the point.

About a millisecond after the words were out of my mouth, his lips crashed down on mine. We kissed and kissed and kissed, and I tingled deep and was seriously on the edge of coming from a kiss alone when a throat being cleared loudly finally made me pull back and break apart from the most amazing lips on God's green earth.

It was Montgomery, standing at the bottom of the steps, a smile on his face as he looked at us. "It's all over. VanDoren Enterprises has been sold."

Sully took my hand and led me over to him. "How did it all shake out? Who owns my father's legacy?"

Montgomery smiled wider. "I do."

Sully took a step back, and I could see by his face he was not happy. "I didn't take you for a back-stabbing son of a—"

Montgomery rolled his eyes. "I bought it so I could manage it and hold it in trust for your sister until she comes of age, dipshit."

Sully's tense body immediately relaxed. He let go of my hand only so he could throw his arms around his friend in a violent hug. It was brief, but by the look in both of the men's eyes when they came apart, I could tell it was meaningful to both of them.

"Thank you, brother," Sully said.

Montgomery nodded. "Always."

"So that's it?" Sully said. "I just get to walk away scot free?"

"Well, you don't get to be a member if that's what you're asking."

Sully laughed bitterly. "Oh no, I don't get to run around in a cloak and scare poor women who are being chased down like dogs and thrown in coffins? Sorry, pal, that's your gig, not mine. I'll be happy to put this fucking manor in my rearview and never look back."

Montgomery visibly cringed at that bit, but Sully didn't take it back. I knew Sully was still plenty pissed about all the cruel things I'd had to suffer while under that roof and on these grounds. Really, I couldn't imagine Sully as part of the Order.

Montgomery leaned in, a furrow in his brow. "That's too bad because I'm trying to change the Order from the inside, and I could have used a good man like you."

But Sully just shook his head. "I don't have the patience for that bullshit. I see something fucked up, I want to break it, not remake it."

Montgomery nodded, probably wisely choosing not to pursue this battle any further.

But then Sully hugged him again hard and I faintly heard his words whispered in Montgomery's ear. "But thank you, brother. You'll always have my gratitude for what you've done today. Nothing will ever change that."

When they broke apart, I could tell Montgomery was moved but trying to hide it. He cleared his throat again but then jammed a thumb over his shoulder back at the manor. "Well, I better get back. They're drawing up the paperwork as we speak."

"And the kidney?" I piped up, needing the extra assurance. "It's really on its way to Reba?"

Montgomery smiled. "They're prepping her for surgery now."

I grabbed Sully's hand. "Oh my God, we have to go! We'll barely be able to make it back in time!"

Sully called goodbye to Montgomery over his shoulder as I dragged him back towards Sully's truck for the twenty-minute drive back to the hospital.

He kept a soothing hand on my knee, rubbing small circles of comfort the entire way there.

The End

Want to read a bonus scene of Reba's welcome

home party from Rafe's point of view, where he
meets an old high school flame?
Click here now to read the bonus scene!

Don't stop reading yet.
The Breaking Belles series continues with
Opulent Obsession
Are you ready for Rafe Jackson's story?

Forbidden

For all of my books, check out my Amazon Page!

http://amzn.to/2CTmeen

ALSO BY STASIA BLACK

DARK CONTEMPORARY ROMANCES

BREAKING BELLES SERIES

Elegant Sins

Beautiful Lies

Opulent Obsession

Inherited Malice

Delicate Revenge

Lavish Corruption

DARK MAFIA SERIES

Innocence

Awakening

Queen of the Underworld

Innocence Boxset (Boxset)

BEAUTY AND THE ROSE SERIES

Beauty's Beast

Beauty and the Thorns

Beauty and the Rose

Billionaire's Captive (Boxset)

Theirs To Ransom

Marriage Raffle Boxset (Boxset)

ABOUT STASIA BLACK

STASIA BLACK grew up in Texas, recently spent a freezing five-year stint in Minnesota, and now is happily planted in sunny California, which she will never, ever leave.

She loves writing, reading, listening to podcasts, and has recently taken up biking after a twenty-year sabbatical (and has the bumps and bruises to prove it). She lives with her own personal cheerleader, aka, her handsome husband, and their teenage son. Wow. Typing that makes her feel old. And writing about herself in the third person makes her feel a little like a nutjob, but ahem! Where were we?

Stasia's drawn to romantic stories that don't take the easy way out. She wants to see beneath people's veneer and poke into their dark places, their twisted motives, and their deepest desires. Basically, she wants to create characters that make readers alternately laugh, cry ugly tears, want to toss their kindles across the room, and then declare they have a new FBB (forever book boyfriend).

Join Stasia's Facebook Group for Readers for access to deleted scenes, to chat with me and other fans and also get access to exclusive giveaways:

Stasia's Facebook Reader Group

Want to read an EXCLUSIVE, FREE novella, Indecent: a Taboo Proposal, that is available ONLY to my newsletter subscribers, along with news about upcoming releases, sales, exclusive giveaways, and more?

Get **Indecent: a Taboo Proposal**

When Mia's boyfriend takes her out to her favorite restaurant on their six-year anniversary, she's expecting one kind of proposal. What she didn't expect was her boyfriend's longtime rival, Vaughn McBride, to show up and make a completely different sort of offer: all her boyfriend's debts will be wiped clear. The price?

One night with her.

Website: stasiablack.com

Facebook: facebook.com/StasiaBlackAuthor

Twitter: twitter.com/stasiawritesmut

Instagram: instagram.com/stasiablackauthor

Goodreads: goodreads.com/stasiablack

BookBub: bookbub.com/authors/stasia-black

ABOUT ALTA HENSLEY

ALTA HENSLEY is a USA TODAY bestselling author of hot, dark and dirty romance. She is also an Amazon Top 100 bestselling author. Being a multi-published author in the romance genre, Alta is known for her dark, gritty alpha heroes, sometimes sweet love stories, hot eroticism, and engaging tales of the constant struggle between dominance and submission.

As a gift for being my reader, I would like to offer you a FREE book.
DELICATE SCARS
Get your copy now! ~
https://dl.bookfunnel.com/tnpuad5675

Join Alta's Facebook Group for Readers for access

to deleted scenes, to chat with me and other fans and also get access to exclusive giveaways:
Alta's Private Facebook Room

As a gift for being my reader, I would like to offer you a FREE book.

DELICATE SCARS

Get your copy now! ~

https://dl.bookfunnel.com/tnpuad5675

Check out Alta Hensley:

Website: www.altahensley.com

Facebook: facebook.com/AltaHensleyAuthor

Twitter: twitter.com/AltaHensley

Instagram: instagram.com/altahensley

BookBub: bookbub.com/authors/alta-hensley

Sign up for Alta's Newsletter:

readerlinks.com/l/727720/nl

Made in the USA
Las Vegas, NV
09 December 2020

12477327R00164